QUESTUS

THE BATTLE FOR REALITY

SHAWN WILLIAMSON

CFI
BOOKS

SPECIAL THANKS

The
Monastery
MANCHESTER

This edition published by CFI Books 2024

ShawnWilliamson.com

First published in the United Kingdom in 2024 by CFI Books

CFI R&D Limited trading as CFI Books

27 John Smeaton Court, Manchester, M1 2NR

ISBN 978-1-7391019-8-5

Edited by Anthony Johnson
Editorial Assistance by Lois Stevenson
Typeset by Anthony Johnson
Book Cover Design by Nathan Newman

QUESTUS

The Battle for Reality

Shawn Williamson

Contents

"Wrong will be right, when Aslan comes in sight,

At the sound of his roar, sorrows will be no more,

When he bares his teeth, winter meets its death,

And when he shakes his mane, we shall have spring again."

C.S. Lewis

To those who Quest for a better world...

London England March 2022

Tower Bridge

Before dawn when the day is dead of noise, the scraping sound returned like the scratching of fingernails down a tombstone. Angus MacWilliam dared not look up from his makeshift bed for he already knew what it was. The ashen-marbled hand lived and what haunted him more was that this was a premonition of things to come. If you can imagine the large hands of Leonardo da Vinci, hands which could both bend horseshoes and paint great works like his Christ Salvator Mundi, then you would know that this was his hand.

Angus closed his eyes knowing that the bible verse would be ready for him to read at first light. It was only in the light that he dared to look at the vellum sheets of his bible. Sighing in the darkness, he recalled Leonardo da Vinci's last words to God as he ascended to heaven. "Have I not done enough?" reminding him that the greatest amongst us are often the most humble.

The River Thames washed against Angus's worn-out shoes as he lay in his granite den under Tower Bridge. There was an all-powerful feeling of impending doom. Angus had felt the same in that other world, now just a hazy memory from another time. But deep down, he was aware of things continuing to go wrong in this world. Not just wrong, but distinctly evil.

He got out of his all-weather sleeping bag and went to look at his ancient bible opened by da Vinci's hand and underlined by thin lines of blood. It lay open at the book of Daniel.

1

Angus was safely hidden in his refuge from both the marked and unmarked street people. Times were changing and real danger loomed everywhere. The lapping waters brought back memories reminding him of his time spent far away in that other place, on that fabled Isleta in South America. This had brought him to the City of Light, the most magnificent stone civilisation created by Templars and their allies, the Pirate Brethren.

He knew another portal was coming soon to relieve him of the great test of poverty and penance he had faced. Angus had endured the dark night of the soul…now he was nearly ready.

A Previous Visit to Loch Eriboll

Providentially his one real friend 'in the great chain of the living and the dead', Angela Kirkbride was back. Some years earlier, Angus had travelled with Angela to the Neolithic moon observatory above the mysterious Loch Eriboll in the North of Scotland. Angus remembered back to their journey, beginning symbolically with four huge stags thundering through the heather below a touching monument to HMS Hood. It was years before the great world event, known as 'Earth Change', had happened.

Large white painted stones spelt out the name 'HMS Hood', stark against the brown winter tones on their walk together up the mountain rising above the Loch. HMS Hood was sunk in WW2 by the German Navy. She went down with over a thousand British Navy personnel. The Hood like other British vessels would often anchor out in the deep sea of Loch Eriboll. As Angus would discover the most important thing to manifest would be another German U-Boat. In fact, it was the sister Submarine to the one he'd been involved with in Chile, in that other place, if he could only just remember.

At the end of World War 2, German Kriegsmarine Officers including Admiral Junkers surrendered with thirty-three U-Boats in Loch Eriboll. Angus knew there was more to this than met the eye. Especially as the megalithic Wheelhouse structure was a portal into that other place. It was a place which remained an intermittent memory connected to his work as a Grail Knight. The enigmatic Wheelhouse observatory was a simple structure of stones built as a shelter enabling ancient races to calculate the cycle of the moon. Some said that the wandering tribes of Israel, sometimes described as the Diaspora

Hebrews, travelled to Scotland. Here they built and arranged such monoliths to observe the passage of the moon around the Earth to determine the date of the 'Feast of the Passover' and other sacred dates on their calendar. Strewn around the Wheelhouse structure were much bigger stones. It was as if there had once been a smaller type of Stonehenge which had collapsed during some massive geophysical trauma. Sometimes he wondered how mankind would progress to a higher state of understanding about the universe to improve how people lived harmoniously on Earth. One group though was determined to destroy the planet if they could not control every aspect of it. Now they'd exposed themselves and their intent for the world to see. Which reminded Angus of the biblical text "You shall know them by their works." He had come to know these enemies of God as the New Babylonians and however hard people tried not to see what was happening, they would know the truth, because their own compliance to the chain of events leading to their world domination had enabled it.

Now Angela, his previous Scottish exploration walking mate, was back in apocalyptic London. She was on her way with some old clothes for him as living on the streets of London had been hard on Angus. He was underweight and reduced to rags by his situation. If he was lucky Angela might bring the tracksuit as well. She'd mentioned that there was a fat man who had died in her apartment block. A man who had lived an unusual life; a life he'd chosen to keep silent about. He'd been a man who'd chosen to do many things in the world and correct many wrongs, choosing to remain silent about what he'd accomplished. And then, like many, he'd succumbed to an unexpected illness. His old clothes had been left outside his door when they were clearing his apartment out. Angela had them washed. She'd often tried to help the man by making him sandwiches or bringing him his

4

medication. But in the end, it was all too late. Curiously there was a touch of Angus about the man. Perhaps that was what intrigued Angela about him. But perhaps there was more to the situation than met the eye.

Returned to London

Angus checked the old analogue phone Angela had given him and thought about her kindness. He had struggled to get himself together again but at least he was off the whisky. For almost a year, he'd been wandering about the streets of London, doing odd jobs in public houses, clearing tables or mopping floors and lining up in soup kitchens. He warmed his bones on the many braziers or open fires, where those who'd lost everything gathered together only to be arrested or force marked. Many people had started to fight back against the street markers, attacking them when there was no escape route. Recently, near Bow Bells in the East End of London, a Hogarthian fight had ensued like no other involving thousands of protestors. A police horse was turned over and its rider captured whilst the officer's mount was killed, butchered and barbequed for essential meat, feeding many. In certain designated poor areas people woke up to the reality of government door knockers requesting confirmation of their marked status. Those that declined to be marked could be taken into custody or sent to the organ recycling factories also known as the end-of-life terminals. Death came for many of them, whilst soothing music played and morphine was administered to ease their passing. Then their bodies were processed for harvesting of their good organs. In these places those who had nothing to offer would be liquidated for fertilisers to feed the compliant with genetically modified produce which made them sick. Most people learned to accept what was happening until it was their turn to be forced into the end-of-life factories. They complained or moaned and sometimes had tantrums. But never did it occur to them that what was happening was abysmal.

Because they couldn't imagine that one day they'd be next. And when their day came it was simply too late.

This subterfuge of mayhem functioned alongside engineered social behaviours to create a morass of immorality through some unfathomable force. It was a way to control people by putting them in a jail of the mind devoid of their spiritual source. Humanity was being purposefully dumbed down and London was the place where the New Babylonians were preparing their new world capital. You see, London had become an Independent Corporate State, no longer part of the British Isles.

It was in Angus's nature to rebel against all that was not for the good, because 'what is born of the bone can never be driven from the blood'. And that's why he'd been chosen as an agent of God despite his problems. He knew he'd come from that other place connected to his past life as a Grail Knight but his test required him to prove himself in more than one dimension.

The morning had arrived. From his granite den Angus looked out across the Thames where London was waking up. Boats pushed barges past the Albert Embankment carrying passengers or freight. A harbour tugboat attached itself to a steel barge clinking together echoing over the grey waters. Billows of smoke puffed from its funnel as the blast from its melancholy horn echoed around.

Shoeless, Angus rinsed his face and feet in the river ready to meet with Angela under the steps. His den was warm and had given him some protection from the elements. Strangely it was rat free down under the bridge. Angus sometimes thought of the rats and how they were like a barometer of the state of humanity. He'd once laughed at his wife in that other world for allowing the rats to co-exist in the roof of their

7

house, in return for them keeping away from the area where they would eat. That was the way of the new age people in South America. They thought they had power over nature. Angus was getting more and more visions from the other place. But the rats were back in force in London now bigger and stronger than ever before.

At the back of the den under London Bridge Angus kept his precious possessions in a rucksack including the wooden Grail bowl. Angus knew there was a purpose for him having it and one which would reveal itself again soon. Sometimes he had recollections of when he'd discovered it in 1160 in the Temple of Solomon. To add to his confusion his great mentor and guide Dr Andrew Sinclair had disappeared again. One day Angus returned to where Andrew's apartment overlooked the Thames only to find it was undergoing refurbishment and boarded shut.

"Hello, are you down there?" Angus looked up to see Angela standing stylishly in her morning breakfast outfit. She was made-up wearing an activity style racing combination with stripes down the leggings, carrying an Italian handbag under one arm and holding a bundle of clothing and some trainers under the other. She was a London lady through and through. There had been some early history between them, but that was in a secular world of sun and crisp Italian wine when they'd been in Rome researching the cold marble tombs. Angus had felt a previous connection to a marble sepulchre in Rome where biblical heroes were said to be buried. Despite trusting Angela he'd often experienced two sides to her. It was like there was another robust version of her trying to get out and do exciting things on the planet.

"I've got the clothes and trainers for you, come on out, you can grow into the track suit as you build yourself up again. It might be a bit big," Angela said looking at the massive green track suit.

"Och Lassie I am no' tha' bad, just need a few good meals and some gym exercise to build me up again, och' we've been doing ok right enough," he replied gaunt faced and high cheek boned.

Squinting, Angus looked up into the bright morning light. He held out his arms to receive his new clothes. Angela dropped them down the steps and he caught them.

"Thanks Lassie, you'll notice I've washed ma' feet and had a shave."

"Come on put the track suit on and let's get some breakfast," Angela said holding her mobile phone to her ear distracted by a conversation she was having with her cleaner. Angus rooted through the clothes putting the rags he was wearing into a plastic bag. Bewildered he pulled on the track suit bottoms and put on the top.

"Did ya' bring them trainers wi' ya?"

"Yes, come on there's everything you need, come on! I don't want to miss the reservation."

"Ah fa' crying out loud Lassie, it's only a feckin' bowl of soup we are going for."

"Come on you daft Scotsman, I don't want to upset them." But Angus was distracted by something.

"Jesus, Mary and Joseph I canna' believe what I am seeing, ya' beauty! It's a Hibernian tracksuit, what are the chances of that!" Angus cried out. "Look at that, it's got the logo on and everything, and in Hibernian green. Och' it's a bit baggy but when I fill out again, it'll be right enough and this is ma' team Lassie!" he said puffing his chest out.

9

He laced up his trainers and splashed on some cheap aftershave. He took a belt and tightened it to pull up the slack in the bottoms. He grabbed his rucksack with the Grail in it and climbed up the stone steps opposite the Embankment to face Angela. Curiously the granite which had afforded him shelter was somehow warm to the touch instead of cold and numbing. But it was warm as if Angus's presence had unwittingly activated an unknown energy within its matrix. For some reason he had liked to take his shoes off and hold his bare feet in the sand and gravel on the edge of the River Thames. It charged him up somehow.

"Come on now Lassie, don't let me distract ya'." Angela was still on her mobile phone.

"Yes please that's all good, just finish the bathroom and make the guest bedroom ready," she said clicking off the conversation abruptly.

She turned to Angus giving him her full attention. "Nice track suit by the way, it's a bit big but it suits you," she added, pleased with his reaction.

"Och' Lassie, the bonus is they're ma' Hibernian colours," he said head creased with lines of expectation. "What are the chances of that?"

Angela pouted, "Football is not my thing! I wouldn't know one team from the other. Now if they'd been Gucci colours that's another story."

"Ya would na' be saying that if you'd have seen George Best in those Hibs colours. That was some spectacle to see as a young'en." Angus drifted back to his young drinking days down in Leith before he set out with the Hib's casuals for Easter Road.

Angela set off briskly for the Japanese breakfast place. Angus caught her up. Cohorts of people were out walking in their masks of compliance defining them as 'gone over' to the great re-setters. Fear was now the new driver rumbling through the sewers and streets of London. The maskers as Angus had called them sought relief from the constant mental trauma perpetrated against them by the government if you could call them that.

"Och' Lassie da' na' mind them. They da' na' know what they're doing. They just do as they're told."

Angela kept her head down gliding towards their reserved table. Angus removed his rucksack and carefully sat down on a chair marked 'made from recycled wood', but it wasn't, it was plastic.

"It's ma' time to pay Lassie, you've been buying for the last two weeks."

"No Angus you pay when you've got money, that's what this is all about and you can't even get unemployment benefit."

"Aye Lassie you've got to be on the register of the marked for that."

Angela looked down the Embankment at the unfolding spectacle of London under the New Babylonians. Angus hadn't finished.

"I beg to differ ma' Lady, a' danna' need anything now." Angus said reaching into his rucksack. "Look what I found stitched into the lining of the rucksack!"

He held his hand shut so she couldn't see what he was holding. Just as the waiter came over to take their order, he opened his hand.

"I found this, it's a bit weird right enough. It was just stitched in the secret compartment in the rucksack. But I canna' remember how it came to be in ma' keeping."

Angus opened his hand and the sunlight caught the gold signet ring sending an explosion of yellow blaze so powerful even the waiter dropped his order book shielding his eyes with his hand. Angela did the same as the supernatural light flashed before her eyes as well. Settling down Angela put her sunglasses on staring at the ring. It had a satellite of rubies circling a Knights Templar cross v-cut into the gold casing. Around the perimeter of the ring was a snake consuming itself in a figure of eight.

"Oh my God Angus where did that come from?" Angus put it away.

"Look Lassie there's na' way that ring is for sale. I'll explain more about it later. The thing is it came wi' these beauties!" Angus held his hand out showing Angela the two gold coins. "They came out of the rucksack as well." He said winking. Angela looked them over.

"Wow! I think your credit rating has just gone up! They look like gold doubloons," she said smiling. Dealing in antiquities and precious jewellery was how Angela had made her money. And often it was Angus's historical explorations which had afforded her opportunities she would not normally have had.

Angus grinned. "Got ta' be worth a few grand."

The waiter came back, he could see the ring which had caused the bright flash and stayed well back.

"Are you having the usual the both of you?"

Angela apologised to him. "Sorry about that bright flash it nearly blinded me as well!" The waiter rubbed his eyes squinting. Angela pulled down her sunglasses repeating her order. "We would like the lime juice and a large coffee with the eggs and prawns as well and of course the fish soup," Angela requested. She was endeavouring to build Angus up again as he'd lost muscle tone merely surviving under London Bridge. If only Angela had known sooner. She'd owed Angus a favour from days gone by. But things were not so one sided as they appeared.

Nodding frantically the waiter walked back towards the food preparation area.

"Please pay attention Angus. You know you can stay with me for the next few days etc."

"Och there's no need Angela. I think 'am on the mend. Last night, I had a vision. I was standing in the Templar Chapel in London looking for something sacred carved in the stone. It's not coincidental tha' the vision came after I discovered the Templar ring." Angela drifted back to their time together in Rome. What Angus had said in his sleep had frightened her as he ranted about a call to arms to fight demons down in underground ice tunnels. He cursed the King of the Demons, Agrimas seven times. She remembered the number seven.

"Perhaps you're needed again? Maybe it's time to get a job over at the Temple as a stonemason. Do they still need them?" Angela knew there was a golden seam of truth running through Angus's interpretation of the world. But sometimes she was just like everyone else unwilling to confront fragmented reality. Demon armies and the Holy Grail wasn't a major talking point for the majority of the consuming population. In fact, people were happier in their bubbles of compliance. Angela was a good person and Angus had once saved her from the ravages of poverty by helping her become a millionaire. And what Angela didn't know about selling wasn't worth knowing.

"What about getting some stonemason's work over at the Temple?" she said again.

"Na' Lassie, not anymore, the globalist's danna' want our national culture. Ya' know our country isn't the same as it was." Angus scowled, "It's all about the coming of the Great World Government with people doing as they are told with the comin' satanic Artificial Intelligence robot people. Aye and them devils would rather turn us into robots. And besides you have to take the mark and ya' know I'll never do that." Angus looked up to the sky exploring the clouds with his eyes. "If I could remember clearly where I come from' I'd av' gone back straight away."

Angela put her sunglasses back on top of her head. Angus could see her eyes flickering and telegraphing her deep concerns. Everyone knew what was happening; it was the unspeakable truth which many dare not think about. The coming world was supposed to be where New Babylonian elites would become gods over the only God.

Another group of fully masked people glided past. Even the kids were wearing them. The masks acted in most cases as visual symbols of those who were willingly compliant.

"For feck' sake they gonna' suffocate dem' kids."

Just forget it all Angus. You've got to get back into the Temple, it's calling you!"

Then an intense dizziness came over Angus and Angela. Angus's eyes rolled showing more white than normal.

"Agh' wha' was that? Fa' feck sake I nearly passed out." Angus steadied himself holding the chair. "Remember that force field on the way to the moon observatory at the Wheelhouse above Loch Eriboll? That place if you can call it that, where we both nearly passed out?" Angus said.

"I've never forgotten those mega stones buzzing with wild energy, one could almost see them living. It held us for a time in some other place. But I really want to return, it was so wonderful and such a sense of the profound." Angela said brushing away a pesky fly.

"Aye, and the sense of falling asleep on our feet up there! Living a lifetime in the blink of an eye. I've not finished with that place yet. I'm gonna' be going back there soon! It's another portal like Rosslyn I just know it." Sometimes Angus recounted events linked to his purpose as a Grail Knight but in essence they were actually premonitions revolving through time like a roulette wheel.

The Plastic Death Trees

Looking down the Embankment, cohorts of masked people stopped and looked up into the sky. Eerily, they were all fixed on the same spot on top of a building over on the other side of the Thames. Munching their food some of the other diners gawped in that direction as well. They looked vacuously at a large transmitter disguised in the shape of a tree that was clearly fake plastic, just like the models of motionless birds sat amongst the fabricated branches. Once a month, in the dead of night, government contract cleaners appeared in special suits to wash the fake tree and clear away the dried-up dead birds killed by its abysmal electromagnetic frequency. The EMF trees like the thousands of surveillance cameras on the streets were always installed in the dead of night.

Angela said, "for God's sakes look! They're like bloody zombies, starring up at the plastic tree!"

"Aye a' ken', they're turning into zombies." Mockingly Angus walked jerkily like an automaton drawing attention to himself. Angus's robotic movements were so realistic some of the 'rubber neckers' were distracted from starring at the fake tree to watch him. Angus carried on "Aye come on then ya' gorpers, you'll be like this soon enough!"

"Stop it Angus people are watching!"

All the time something was happening to the people and how they were living, changing for the worse. Angela had researched electromagnetic frequency or EMF and how it could be used to change brain waves rendering people into compliant automatons. They'd already done that with TV personalities programming them to read what they were told without questioning. As we know from history those who don't question governments' narrative are destined to be subject to it. 'Trust the science' was the fast track to the graveyard. But the ignorant implementers of such unquestionable policy were only interested in profit, for they put profit before God.

Trembling, the waiter came back just as everyone's dizziness and ringing ears stopped.

"Sorry, I can't seem to remember what you ordered?" he said looking blank.

"Ya' wrote it down man!"

"Shush' Angus I'll deal with it," Angela interjected with motherly tones.

The disorientation caused by the electromagnetic frequency tree mast had caused the waiter to blank out. Angela reached out for his customer order book. Compassionately she took it from him gently tucking her hair behind her ear looking down at what the waiter had written. He'd taken their order and then forgotten it.

"Look the order is here!" she said pointing down at what the waiter had written. The waiter came over ashen faced and began to read it. "Large coffee, lime juice, poached eggs, prawns and two bowls of the Japanese fish soup.

"Er' sorry looks like I wrote it down after all."

"Aye Lad, alright then, the order is coming outta' the kitchen anyways," Angus said feeling the smooth skin on his chin after shaving his beard off under London Bridge with a disposable razor.

"By the way, a' ken' you from the soup kitchen over near the Embankment underground station." The waiter didn't respond looking away. More and more people were on the poverty line, struggling to get enough food.

"Angus they don't understand what 'a' ken'' means down here. You are a long way from Leith here you know."

"A' ken' Lassie." Angus replied defiantly.

Another waiter came out of the kitchens with their order though. The second waiter put the tray on their table. "Here we are, sorry about that, bon appetit."

There was a further silence as both waiters walked away together pace for pace like they were tied together in an egg and spoon race. Angus meant well; he just couldn't see the point of people working but never being able to make enough money to survive. That was why many workers in London were now lining up for free soup or standing at food banks. The people had been zombified by propaganda into accepting the deadly situation, but the beast system, as he called it was beginning to unravel. And there was the problem of more and more people losing their jobs to Artificial Intelligence. Now Angus saw these well-dressed people standing in line with the down and outs. And he noticed they wore the same clothes over and over. They too were becoming street people.

"You see what I mean," Angela said. "The people are acting like zombies. The so-called government's practicing at it now which can only mean they are close to getting ready. The New Babylonians are ramping up." Angela re-applied some lipstick. "You've got to get into the Temple and remember what you are supposed to be doing, not that I've got a bloody clue," she said pouting glossy red lips.

Angus ate his prawns and fish thinking all the time about the Temple near London's Fleet Street. It had once been the main HQ of the Knights Templar in London. He'd been there many times before and he'd be returning soon. Angela began to eat her food and drink the lime juice whilst the soup steamed from the bowls on the table.

The Beast System Tightens

Both Angus and Angela would never comply by taking 'the mark' as it was named on the streets. The mark was, in fact, the system which connected people to a super Artificial Intelligence called Saturn, designed to control every person on the planet. Saturn could manipulate its victims by withholding the basic necessities of life. Infernally each person would be given a computerised file which would record their every move. If they contravened the rules then they could be starved or put in the work camps and worse; for those who did not comply were destined for the recycling centres.

There had been similar attempts to control humanity by totalitarian regimes in the past. In the UK the battle was still on to assert the 'Beast System' as Angus had called it. Mankind's natural Sovereign Rights issued through Magna Carta were slipping away, as the beast system tightened its grip and people were educated and programmed to be ignorant of their own rights. The people's original human rights had been brokered in the favour of the people by the Knights of the Temple and the Marshal family. William Marshal the Senior, was the greatest Knight in British history. The truth, honour and justice of the Magna Carta was famous throughout the world. Despite this, the general population were sleepwalking away from it to their own nemesis. But Angus believed that he could reinstate a new code of chivalry back into the country. It was just a matter of time; a matter of God's time.

The one thing which protected Angus from the mark system had been his homeless obscurity. Angela had refused the marking procedure that was being pushed like fast food burgers by the new governance centres in the pay of the New Babylonians. Each day another rule and tightening of the screw of tyranny were brought against the people. It was the drip feed of death.

But Angela was rich, and the rich had been accustomed to be more powerful than the poor, it was ever so. Each week the phone calls from her health centre's surgery grew in urgency, imploring her to 'come and get the mark', until she'd found a government source to buy her fake 'marked status'.

Angus was forced to hide away from the marker teams by living under the bargeman steps beneath London Bridge. He lived a twilight life, emerging only at certain safe times. Hundreds of street marker operatives in their orange security overalls and masks of compliance roamed London searching for the unmarked to get their bonus payments. The process started with street marker teams coercing the unmarked to get the mark using emotional pressure and bribes of money or food. Unmarked people were easily identified by a simple bar code reader. It was not uncommon to see people being pinned to the floor screaming as the mark was forced upon them. Severe penalties existed for those who resisted. Panther like, Angus avoided them. The government forced mandatory mask wearing on every person but not themselves; the rules were for the emerging slave class only. Many people just wore them to telegraph what side they were on, merely as an act of subservience known as virtue signalling, which only delayed the inevitable. Government propaganda told people that wearing masks would stop all manner of germs spread from the explosion of rats and other plagues. But the masks were really a social engineering experiment. It started by enforcing compliant people to wear a mask which would cover their nose and mouth. Over time the 'powers that be', including the Global Health Services, changed the shape of the masks so they just covered a person's mouth. Then a new mask was introduced which didn't cover the face at all. In fact, it was more of a halter than a mask. It was tied at the sides and pulled a person's head down tilting their head, encouraging the wearer to look down. The people were told that this was a way of avoiding germs. But the real reason was enshrined in the latest protocols of the New Babylonians. And that was that no member of the slave caste should ever be permitted to look their masters in the face.

The newly appointed enforcers of small rules and acts of compliance were clamping down on everything. They issued traffic and litter tickets and had been carefully recruited from the basest of society. More and more of these types of people were being drafted into the diminishing ranks of the police who had stopped serving the people long ago. The system exemplified the worst traits in its servants.

The Orange Slave Caste

As time went by the uniform of the New Babylonians slave caste developed to include the halter masks, a security bracelet medallion which informed others of their marked status and a set of baggy orange overalls which looked similar to those worn by prisoners. By complying and taking the mark, slaves would be given tokens for the new food developed from alternative sources including insect and waste human protein. It was much easier for people to accept the inevitability of eating human protein once they were re-conditioned to not believe in a divine being. And now the main purpose of the media and the church was to get the people to abandon belief in God. They would simply replace God with the Saturn Computer which would run the people and their AI clones. In some, as yet unknown way, many human's life force was being fused with technology turning them into a prototype subhuman species. Already newly changed humans were enshrined in New Babylonian legislation. And they would be rewarded by entering the ranks of the elite's slave caste. It was all part of the great plan disguised as the fourth Industrial Revolution.

Being 'marked' was carried out by tattooing a blue luminescent mark on the right hand or forehead of the receiver enabling them to get food warmth and shelter.

Angus had something on his mind. "Let's take a jog over to ware' Andrew Sinclair lived. It will be good exercise."

"But I thought you said his apartment block had been closed?" Angela said.

"Aye I did, but maybe something changed."

Angela knew something of Dr Andrew Sinclair and had even met him once in a different phase of her life. His parties had once been the talk of the socialites in London but that had been in the better times of social grace.

"By the way, I found a place which will exchange your gold coins for cash! Then you could get a prepaid credit card or something. You know what it's like for cash these days."

"Aye so I do Lassie, ya' know there's still many exchanging cash. Nothing beats that flow of freedom from a good ol' twenty quid note rustling its way over the bar."

Gold and Cash into Credit Cards

Angela tapped into the web to get an approximate valuation of the doubloons. "Look here, the nearest and best value is about £1,600. So that will be the lowest we'll take", she said pointing at the screen of her phone looking curiously at Angus. "You know I still don't know how you came by those gold pieces. It's such a mystery." Angus knew what she was thinking. Angela was wondering if he'd robbed them just because he was down and out. She could be a bit that way.

"Ya' should limit the use of that phone and the internet they're knocking out more and more radiation ya' know."

"Angus love, we have to function in the modern world!"

Angus paid the bill with loose cash he'd borrowed from Angela, they didn't like it, but it was that or nothing. They strode off down toward the Houses of Parliament also known as the 'Place of Lies' which had been changed now so that it appeared stark white in the rising morning heat of London. The scaffolding, where Babylonian contractors had been installing white marble, was being taken down as they looked on. The main tower where 'Big Ben' was housed was still covered in sheeting. The time was drawing close to revealing the statues of the New Babylonians gods. Already the New Babylonians had decided they wanted their elite buildings clad in marble decorated with gold leaf. The marble used was quarried from where Babylon had existed in the Middle East. And that was the main reason dealers like Zove's had sprung up buying gold in exchange for the preferred pre-paid credit. Gold was the mortar between the bricks of the culture of New

Babylon. It was used to decorate and featured in their diabolic rituals and they worshipped it.

The policy was that all culture and heritage from old Britain would be phased out to make way for culture derived from the opulent extravagance of the elites. It all sounded grand; it was just a question of changing the frame of what the people had previously been used too. And the New Babylonians had recruited regiments of social scientists to help them brainwash people. The main trait of all who served the New Babylonians was the lure of high pay to the ones who did their bidding and eventually this was the route to self-destruction.

Angus and Vanessa walked round the bow in the River Thames heading along the river walk. Other people walked about in an everyday way or at least that was what it seemed. Something was wrong though. Although they behaved as normal, they seemed almost soulless, like their life force was diminished and deflated like old flat tyres. After taking the mark the people were like old worn cars. It was like they'd gone into the compliance garage as a standard reliable car and come out like weary bangers; the people were struggling to keep going.

Giant Rats and Ancient Witches

Giant rats were being reported all along the River Thames. This rat infestation had increased exponentially in London. Angus watched them scurrying over people's feet with brazen impunity searching for bits of fast food. The rats no longer feared humans as if they recognised they were incapable of harming them in their dumbed down zombie state. Curiously instead of infesting the poor, the rats had developed a taste for the high life. Now they were following the rich from eatery to brasserie to wine bar to high life party, passing on unknown diseases.

In the London plagues during the olden days, people thought the rat problem had been caused by witches and their cats. The people then rampaged about like the villagers in a Frankenstein movie stupidly killing all the cats which they believed were witches in disguise. This ridiculous action removed the rat's major predator, causing half the people in old London to be wiped out by the plague virus, carried by fleas living on the rats. Yet the hardy rats became invulnerable. Now there were not enough rat catchers to make any difference. In fact, strangely the only way to avoid being marked with the electronic chip on the streets of London was to train to become a city rat catcher. The thinking behind this by the powers-that-be was simply that they were aware of the physiological damage the mark was inflicting on the people and they couldn't risk the rat catchers of London being sick like everyone else. That would have been a threat to their existence because the rats were following them about more so than the poor. These large vociferous rodents had developed a taste for the food and lifestyles of the elites.

Such specialised operatives were generally well protected by their own natural immunity. The rat catchers of London had their own union and were allowed to function as long as they did not socialise with anybody from the technocratic state. They operated in the twilight hours when all the elites had left the bars and eateries and had returned to their tower mansions and gated and walled communities. Here they remained safe from the intrusion and chaos around them.

Government Gold Dealers

"You need an appointment to see the Zove gold dealers." Angela phoned ahead to make one. "Yes that's it, 10.30 is fine." There was a pause. "This is Angela Kirkbride and I will be with my security guy," she said looking at Angus.

"I think it's a gold doubloon and I want cash for it." There was a long pause. "Well, we could buy the prepaid credit card but I want a better rate for that!"

They walked on down the Thames. Angus adjusted his tracksuit pulling the bottoms up as they slipped down. He reached into a zipped pocket and discovered something strange in it. He brought it out and it glinted. It was a small silver pendant of King Robert the Bruce brandishing an axe. He recognised it immediately as being exactly the same as he'd given his daughter in that other reality. He would keep it safe, but he could not process the information. It brought him to the point of feeling dizzy again.

"For pity's sake I should have brought a tighter belt." Angela smiled as the two of them walked faster down the path. Angus breathed hard; he was out of shape. Zove's appeared with its gold bullion bar symbol hanging over the front door. They were met by a security man in a large peaked hat. Angela took over.

"Hello, we've got an appointment, this is Angela Kirkbride." The security guard saluted showing his manicured nails and rolex watch. He eyeballed Angus as he followed Angela inside.

"It's alright Angus, I told them you were my security guy," she said as Angus grinned and said aloud, "Aye ya' needn't eyeball me Laddie just coz' ya' got more gold braid than an Argentinean postman." Angela rolled her eyes at Angus and he shut up.

She walked over to the main counter and was met by the owner's daughter. Angela knew the dealer's chat inside out. "Hello Ms Kirkbride let me take a look at your gold coins."

Angus mumbled under his breath, "for feck sake". The dealer took out the customary eyeglass as Angela handed her the Gonzaga doubloon and her eyes lit up.

"Yes, it's a very good example of a Gonzaga Spanish doubloon, but it does have some wear and tear marks. They were very big in South America particularly in Chile, worth around £1,600. I'll offer you £1200," she said tucking her hair behind her ear. Angus watched Mr Zove hovering in the background. Angela spoke, "No, it's not enough. I want £1,600 or I'll try somewhere else." The lady dealer looked over at her father stood in the doorway from behind darkened security glass. "Look I don't mean to be blunt, but we own all the gold dealer outlets. I'll go as high as £1,400 but that's it." She bit her bottom lip succulent with shiny red lipstick. Angus looked crest fallen.

"There's more where that came from." Angela said beckoning Angus with her eyes to give her the other gold pieces. Angus rummaged in the rucksack and brought them out in their plastic container whilst the dealer waited in anticipation. Angela took them from Angus.

"Here we are, this is just the beginning and I'll tell you what, if you give me £1,600 I'll take the amount on the prepaid credit card." Poker faced the dealer looked over to her father, who nodded approvingly whilst taking a pinch of snuff.

"Ok but please come back to Zove gold dealers then and I'll do the credit card for you. And remember, this Zove card is valid anywhere in London."

"Please make the card out to Angus MacWilliam and use the address on my passport she said handing it over."

"That will do fine Ms Kirkbride." She passed over the gold piece whilst Mr Zove the owner came back with the completed Zove credit card. "Great to do business with you, do come back to us with the other doubloons." Then Mr Zove mimicked a pirate by making an O with his thumb and index finger and raising it to his eye to represent a pirate's eye patch saying, "aye Jim Lad" with a big smile. Angus watched curiously and to him it looked more like he was making the sign of the all-seeing symbolic eye used by the New Babylonians. Many had said that the enormous London Big Wheel ride was called 'the London Eye' for the same reason.

Mr Zove hadn't finished, "now if you'll excuse us, we are expecting representatives from the House of Babylon." Mr Zove realised he'd made a mistake. "Er sorry, I mean Parliament."

Angus flushed red with anger and signed the back of the card, he was back in business and at least he'd got something. Angus took the card and put it in the rucksack, leaving the shop with Angela. "Och' aye Parliament ya' say…ya' mean the House of Liars!" he said. The point was that gold was in high demand. They were using gold in the microchip factories, for it was an essential compound for microchips and circuits. Everyone was selling their gold to the agents of New

Babylon. And everyone was supposed to be getting microchipped. The process known as 'marking'. And without it no one could function in this twisted upside-down City of London, warned about in the Bible.

On his way outside Angus started to feel disorientated after a flashback seeing himself again as the Grail Knight. He was slashing at a huge hydra-head in the winter light in tunnels of ice. His sword severed the first lunging head in a welter of blood leaving the other six heads flailing around. Blood poured from its necks eroding his boots which was somehow linked to the fact that he'd been shoeless down in his den under London Bridge. It was as if his destitution had been caused by New Babylonians, symbolising having no shoes as part of his poverty penance.

The Houses of New Babylon

Angela steadied Angus. He pushed through the security door of Zove's out onto river walk pulling at his neck. With all her might she slapped him. There was a resounding clap and Angus returned to the now, feeling like he wanted to throw up. It still wasn't over, for round the corner came the real spectacle somehow linked to his episode like a premonition.

Seven representatives came out, walking together. Democracy had finished after the first phase of the attacks on the people called 'the marking of the herd'. Citizens were no longer elected by the people but directly appointed by the New Babylonians.

Now the Roman idea of distracting the masses, previously played out in their coliseums, called 'bread and games', was being gainfully employed once again to distract the masses of Britain. The purpose was to keep the people engaged with base entertainments like rich living, high-end chef programmes on the television, averting them from the real perils which they would face. Gluttony programmes with purulent fake chefs were all the rage. It was a particularly assiduous situation as most of the real world was starving to death. Gladiatorial combat was back, along with public human and animal sacrifices. It was a theatre of pre-programmed degradation of the people purposefully designed to destroy them from the inside out.

Now a theatrical spectacle of extravagance entered the arena. It was like watching a time travel scene. Angus watched so called 'Members of Parliament' now dressed in fine gold threaded silk of Babylonian officials. Their beards were crimped and platted and their bodies draped in gold and silver trim and they wore Sinbad rolled up ended shoes. The women wore immaculate finery, and their hair was braided with silk thread. They were being attended by servants with ostrich feather fans and umbrellas to keep them cool and shaded from the bright sun. All wore silk masks as part of their costume. It was a way of elevating themselves identifying them as superior in an elitist way. It was a way of getting the exclusive handle on communication and making it special. Of course, it was the same for the New Babylonian slave caste who were permitted to emulate their masters. Slaves could only wear orange safety face coverings along with high visibility clothing denominating them as subservient.

A young woman resplendent in the furs of endangered species marched in the front of the group carrying an image of a horned deity with silver teeth and twinkling ruby eyes. She lifted high Nergal, their god of plagues and the underworld. Nergal grinned infernally at those who had already died near the park opposite Zove gold dealers. It was known that the New Babylonians were involved in abysmal black magic rituals contrary to the wellbeing of the people. And now all over London they'd been erecting monuments bearing testimony to their draconian plans calling it the fourth industrial revolution. But first they made political attacks on the credibility of Britain's heroes and let the people vandalise them first.

Angus staggered over to the river boundary wall and threw up. When he looked round again wiping his mouth, the New Babylonians were back wearing their ill-fitting conservative suits and dresses. They paid no attention to him or Angela. Angela looked up to the buildings near the plastic EMF tree to see more security snipers. She went over to Angus and eased him through the flood entry barriers out of the way. She felt him shaking with rage.

34

"Wow what's wrong Angus what else did you see?"

"Och' I'll explain later."

"It's strange I just heard on the TV this morning, that they've nearly finished cladding the dull old Parliament buildings with precious marbles and gold leaf to give it a face lift and all. Might look quite attractive and introduce new green spaces all around Westminster." Angela said unaware of the real situation.

"Aye, more like the hanging gardens of blasted' Babylon! They're celebrating turning London into the headquarters of the New Babylonian cult. Nay' wonder I am seeing the slaying of the seven headed hydra which carried the Whore of Babylon! And we know what happened to them don't we?"

And all the bronze and marble statues which had once represented the heroes of Britain had been switched for the gods and elites of Babylon with most people never noticing some of these were Baal, Nergal and Moloch. All were destroyers of people.

Statues of British heroes which once adorned the centre of London had now been deemed offensive and were torn down to make room for the new order of things. Britain was being eaten from the inside out like a victim of a parasitic insect. The country staggered on hypnotised into hosting its own nemesis. People's silence to untold infringement of their rights had all but broken the country. Babylonian mechanisms of control had been installed in all local governments throughout the country and indeed other countries. This new regime ruled their slaves by fear. Angus realised his work was for God. But he'd need to go back where the real warfare would happen in the ice tunnels under Chile on the way to Antarctica, at least for now.

By mid-morning the babble of the voices along the Thames had unexpectedly died away. Something was about to happen. Angus looked down on the ground to see ants carrying a leaf to their entrance into the ground. It appeared to him that several of them were being ridden by miniature humanoids like some kind of magic circus ant farm spectacle.

"What's wrong Angus" Angela said.

"Aw naw' for fecks sakes," Angus said, "feckin' ants being ridden by some kind of people what tha' hell is going on." He thought he was going insane as he often did when he saw similar outlandish visions. The truth was he was having a premonition about events to come.

Andrew Sinclair, Knight Marshal

There was a disturbance along the River Thames as Angus watched people fall to the ground. Some tourists ran over and took action immediately carrying out cardiopulmonary resuscitation on those who lay gagging for breath. They pushed rhythmically on the chests of the dying people. Then armed police arrived in the globalist riot vans. They stormed over and began beating up those people trying to save the lives of those struggling to breath.

"Stay back," a Globalist Officer screamed, "put their masks back on!" he brayed through a riot megaphone. Globalist Officers ran in wearing protective gloves and began to push their masks back on even though several of them were already unconscious. Angus wanted to help them, but Angela pulled him away knowing he was in danger.

"Come on run Angus run! Look at what's happening."

"Och' come on then, let's get over to Andrew's apartment."

The thing was that such violent spectacles occurred on a daily basis.

A Letter from Another Dimension

Rattling the main door, Angus and Angela tried to enter the apartment block where Andrew lived. He wrote his books on the Templars here overlooking the River Thames. Andrew wrote from an octagonal room at the top of the building. The octagon was a geometric shape, revered by the Templars and known to have sacred qualities. But there was much more to him than just this.

The concierge was waiting for them. "Can I help you Sir?" He seemed benign enough but there was more to him as well.

"Och' Laddie you're keen! I just wanted to go up to see Andrew's flat and look at the door for old time's sake. Like a kind of pilgrimage."

"Can I have your name please? Dr Sinclair has been away for some time and we have no intelligence on when he's returning."

"Aye I know the script Laddie, look I am sorry, och' maybe it was a mistake."

Angela put a comforting hand on his shoulder. "It's ok life changes." Angus felt like he was alive in two different dimensions. But the concierge knew who Angus was. In fact, he'd been waiting for him.

"Angus you say?"

"Aye, Angus MacWilliam waiting here in ma' Hibee track suit and fabulous trainers."

"Ah I see now. We've been expecting you Mr MacWilliam. Indeed, we have something for you." The Concierge replied with a superior

38

look walking urgently to his little guard office where all the keys were kept next to the main entrance. He returned with a letter for Angus.

"Tell me where your first port of call was in Scotland?"

"Gi' me tha' letter Laddie, ya' no testing me like a damn schoolteacher!" Angus said thinking back to his disappointing school days up in Thurso, Scotland.

"Not till you answer the question." The caretaker replied determinedly. Although small in stature the concierge had gravitas which was not to be crossed. Angus thought back to try and answer the question. Even when Andrew wasn't here, he still seemed to have some strange power to help him remember things Angus was trying to forget.

Angus looked over at the little pub they'd often gone to when he was in London. It was by chance called the Methuselah Sword. Angus staggered with a sense of foreboding, feeling another neurological episode coming on. His heart raced and he breathed heavily as he remembered back to sacred Rosslyn Chapel.

"Fa' pity sake man it was Rosslyn Chapel, that was ma' first port of call. Only I now know it as a portal!"

Angela stood by him. She'd seen him like this before.

"That's all! We've been waiting for you bonnie Laddie," the caretaker said sardonically and then held out the letter addressed to Angus.

"Can't help you anymore Angus, the rest is up to you," the caretaker said as if he knew him really well. "If you'll excuse me, I've got intriguing dimensions to attend to."

"Did I hear that right Laddie, did you say other dimensions?"

"Yes, I am doing some dimensional drawings and repairs to Andrew's apartment, well at least supervising the contractors there."

"Fa tha' sake of a mental shite ya' doing ma head in!"

Angela gently pulled Angus away from the concierge. She knew what he was thinking. And she knew it was too early for Angus to be taking it further whilst the caretaker went off humming a Gregorian chant. Angus tucked the letter away in his rucksack.

"Come on Angus, let me see it?"

"Nay Lassie I think I need to read it back at your place, if the offer's still open?"

"That's a better option than you going back under the Tower Bridge steps. There's too much trouble about. And I said you could stay till your mission has come into focus."

"I'll tell you what Lassie let's take a cab back to yours and I'll pay with the Zove card." Angus said proudly.

He flagged down a black cab and they crossed the road and got in it right outside the pub, Methuselah Sword. "Bloomsbury please," Angela asserted. Angus took great pride in paying with the Zove credit card. If he'd known who created this card he would have died with shame. There was more to it than just pride. However, strategically the card was a good move for a chess player in the greater scheme of things. Once the card had been activated it was a good cover enabling him to look like he was compliant with the state of things. It would take some of the heat off from the New Babylonians all seeing surveillance in London. He had bought some other things with the card just to make sure. Like boots and expedition equipment in anticipation of his upcoming adventure. Everything was under scrutiny from the Saturn Supercomputer and its technical slave acolytes.

The Grail Legacy

Angela lived not too far away from the Temple in London. She'd been left an expensive apartment in Bloomsbury Square, or so she'd told him. The fact was she was just there; she'd always been there.

Angus paid the taxi like a proud man and they went up to Angela's apartment.

The first thing Angus did after he opened the memo from Andrew Sinclair, was ask to take a bath. "Och' Angela I need a good bath Lassie, it's been ages since I felt properly clean," he said, reading the letter, already instinctively knowing what was in it.

Greetings Quester Angus.

A trusted memo.

Your instruction to return has been confirmed by the following method of prescribed substance.

Details.

Take scrapings from the inside of your wooden Grail bowl; enough to coat the inside of a teaspoon and add them to a hot bath. Stay in the bath for 30 minutes. Then go straight to bed. Drink a glass of Châteauneuf-du-Pape. Then you will know all.

End of message.

Written in the presence of Dr Andrew Sinclair.

Angela looked at Angus in the kitchen. "Yes, take a hot bath Angus it will do you good." She said walking over to the wine rack by her granite worktops where it was room temperature.

"Do ya' not want to see what's in the letter?"

"No I don't, it was meant for you not me," she replied looking at the wine selection. "I am going to have a bottle of vino tonight. Fancy joining me?"

"Och' hen ya' danna' have to ask me that. I'll have a glass with you." He watched her drift over to the rack stretching for a bottle in the middle of the rest. Somehow, he knew which bottle she would choose. He'd known from the time she'd mentioned it. Angus's summoning was in the letter.

"Looks like we're going to have this bottle tonight Angus. It's a Châteauneuf-du-Pape adding a bit of historical context to the situation, especially with your visit coming up to the Temple in London and on the eve of Saint John the Baptist."

Angus smiled. "Ya' know it's like a plan coming together now. Ya' couldn't make this stuff up could ya'? because Châteauneuf-du-Pape was always Andrew's favoured wine of all. A little bit of the better side of the enemies of the Templars shall we say." Grasping his letter firmly he didn't want to say anymore.

Angela uncorked the wine and let it stand, "there's a towel in the cupboard over there," she said nodding towards the designer wardrobes. Angus went to the cupboard holding the rucksack with the Grail bowl in it and got out a towel. He didn't want Angela to see what he was about to do.

"I'll be back after the bath; I won't be long Lassie."

"Yes, just go for it, I've got a feeling you are in the flow so to speak."

"Ya' could be bang on there!" Angus said disappearing.

As soon as he was in the bathroom he started to unpack the Grail bowl. It was the same one Andrew Sinclair had discovered in the underground vaults of Rosslyn Chapel. And of course, the bowl was of far greater antiquity than medieval. And had he but known he would have remembered finding it in the Temple of Solomon when he was the Grail Knight with the Templars. He took it out and placed it in the sink. He took out his penknife and scraped at the darkened wooden surface on the inside of it. Angus knew the bowl had been previously used to drink something special. He scraped gently over its surface removing the top layer of a mould like substance. He scraped enough to coat the internal surface of a teaspoon. He went over and ran the bath. Plumes of steam rose from the silver taps up into the air. He added cold water and when the water was cool enough to get in he stopped the taps.

He removed his Hibernian track suit and laid it over the bed. He went over and delicately took hold of the spoon with the mould like substance on it. He held the spoon over the bath and sprinkled it over the water and got in. The warmth of the water eased his aching body. He waited as his muscles relaxed. Steam rose from the bath and began to flow over him, into his nasal passages. All of a sudden, it was like watching a film as his past life flashed before his eyes, from Rosslyn Chapel to where he'd been adventuring in Chile, South America. He remembered his previous times at Andrew Sinclair's overlooking the River Thames under an Octagonal dome, a geometric shape revered by the Knights Templar. Angus could see himself and Andrew sat talking over a pile of notes and heavy medieval looking books and a bible. Then he remembered back to what he was supposed to have known.

The Templar handed Angus a small dirk with a coin bearing two knights on one horse set into the handle. Angus kissed its razor edge with a sense of relief. "And Angus, know that you will be honoured in the Temple in London. The Knights have ordered that we create your effigy in stone to be there for eternity. And I have to tell you, there's more to this situation than meets the eye. Perhaps for another adventure, for this is one of many." Questus 1 2021

He remembered a Templar from that other place explaining that they were going to honour him with an effigy of himself inside the Temple of London. Then he saw Andrew Sinclair sat in his wingback chair from where he wrote like an apparition. Angus felt wide awake, yet strangely distant as he passed between worlds.

"Now Angus you are not finished yet. Take the Grail bowl to the Temple in London and plug it in to the gap left for it between the praying hands of your effigy. The Grail is the key. Now is the time for you to return and there you will find me." And then poof! Andrew disappeared and Angus came round from the episode, feeling groggy.

Now he was stood fully dressed and the bath was clean and empty and Angela was banging on the bathroom door. Angus starred at himself in the mirror not liking his haggard countenance. Written in the steam in the mirror was the word Questus.

"Angus are you ok in there? Hurry up the wine is ready."

Angus could see deep into the bathroom mirror a great expanse of white like a huge sheet of ice in the reflection. He saw a gaping white mouth of a hole opening and a small army of knights and pirates descending into it on their vessels and the great warship Pegasus. He slapped his face to stop himself remembering. It was too soon but he knew he had to return; God was summoning him back. He drank the wine with Angela keeping the rucksack with the Grail bowl nearby at all times.

"I hope ya comin' over to Fleet Street tomorrow and to the Temple."

"Er' not tomorrow and besides I've shopping to do. I hope you can find some work there. But you've got money now anyway."

"Aye that's for sure Angela, but we need a purpose as well. Anyway, thanks to your dealing with the Zove gold people, ya' know like it was part of the prophetic journey to Andrew's; something else is going on Lassie, it's the summoning again." He couldn't be sure, but he thought his rucksack had moved. But then he was tired and had had his large glass of Châteauneuf-du-Pape.

They clinked their glasses together and finished as the sun went down over the capital. "Poor bastards they da' na' know what's coming next," Angus mumbled under his breath looking out over a changing landscape. He picked up the rucksack and went to bed clutching it.

In the morning when Angus woke, he was still holding the rucksack with the Grail bowl in it. He was grateful for the luxury of the big bed and bath at Angela's place. He got dressed and went downstairs to see her.

"Morning Angus there's some coffee there in the pot. I am going to the gym so I'll come out with you." Angus poured his coffee; it was strong giving him the kick start he liked.

"Och Lassie, I'll let you know how it goes over at the Temple. Ya' never know they might ha' some wuk' for me." But he knew all along that wasn't why he was going there. He didn't want to think about it directly, but he knew he might not be coming back.

"Doesn't matter now Angus you've got the Zove credit card and that Templar ring."

Aye true, but I'd never sell the ring, be like selling ma' soul. It's for another purpose!"

He finished his coffee and gave Angela a hug.

The Knight Concierge Returns

Then there was a beep outside. Angus left Angela's place and went down to the taxi. Unexpectedly, the taxi driver was the concierge from Andrew Sinclair's apartment block down on the Thames.

"Och Laddie it's you again, having to do a bit of moonlighting then?"

"Ah yes Angus we all need a little extra money don't we now." The taxi driver replied knowing already where Angus was to be taken.

Angus sat in the back clutching his rucksack. He'd still got his Hibernian tracksuit on but with a tighter belt round his middle which was much thicker and more comfortable than the other. Oddly the taxi driver had noticed it also.

"That belt looks like you should have a sword hanging from it. Might be a different one this time round."

"Eh Laddie? You might be right, maybe it did once over." And that was the truth. For it was a medieval Clan Gunn sword belt from Scotland of platted leather, tanned through a special process in the mountains near his ancestors' castle. And of course, Angus had heard his comment about the different sword but had glazed over it.

The taxi made its way through the changing landscape of London towards the Strand, where the Templar's Chapel was known simply as Temple. There were very few cars but many more buses and lots of people walking, mostly panting in their masks.

"Glad you don't wear a mask Laddie it looks so sadly compliant to something so very wrong."

"Angus, I have a holographic projection of me wearing one, for the purposes of work shall we say. The general public see this, whilst I most definitely never wear one."

Angus began to laugh. "Brilliant Laddie, stay safe, hahaha."

Angus could feel the energy on the streets changing the nearer they got to the Temple and he felt solemn inside.

"Don't be afraid Angus it's not as bad as you are thinking. Just go with the flow, sometimes we all have to just go with the flow. I sometimes call it the Breath of God."

"Aye thanks Laddie, anyone would have thought you'd been sent to look after me. How did you know I was going to Temple? I never said anything I just ordered a taxi." But Angus already knew he'd been sent to help him get back.

The First Attempt Going Through the Temple Portal

They pulled up outside the circular shaped church known as Temple. The streets and passages of the medieval quarter were strangely deserted. Curiously there was a hazy light around the building like a halo.

Angus got out. "How much do I owe ya?"

"Your money is not required here. It's been paid."

"For God's sake Laddie, that's a bit creepy?"

"I am supposed to remain here until I see you've gone inside the Temple," replied the taxi driver nodding over at the arched door with safety warning tape around it. It jogged a memory of the red safety tape around a specific carving he'd been investigating at Rosslyn Chapel. That place too had been a portal, its memory ever distant.

"Aye Laddie, I know you know more about this situation than meets the eye," Angus said aloud to himself walking towards the arched door at the side of the Temple. Angus glanced back at the taxi which remained in the shadows of the car park. Sure enough, it appeared as if he was wearing a mask sat there in his cab. But as he'd humorously explained that was merely a holographic projection.

As Angus entered the arch door the taxi pulled away. He opened the large creaking medieval door and went inside. There was the familiar smell of spices and death he'd first noticed on Chiloe Island, Chile with that distant memory of the City of Light.

In the centre of the church was a new stone effigy of a knight recumbent with praying hands. It was stark white in the gloom. He'd been told once that one day an effigy would be carved of himself but for a special purpose. Suddenly he knew what he was supposed to do. A thought seared through his mind. He got out the Zove prepaid credit card. If he was going to be going away, perhaps forever, then why not have a few beers or some whisky in one of the pubs next to the Temple. Surely there would be no harm in that. Angus didn't see the halo around the Temple building go out. He'd missed his chance. Naturally he'd wanted to go over to the effigy but didn't. As usual Angus made the wrong decisions at the right time.

He walked back through the medieval door looking over to a public house named the Gorgon's Head. He was unaware that it was a dangerous place particularly as it had been created as test facility for Artificial Intelligence. Yet there he was, walking towards it in his Hibernian tracksuit. If he'd been in a Fulham tracksuit, things might have gone better for him. The medieval door closed behind him. He tried the handle again as he turned towards the Gorgon's Head pub. The Temple door had locked him out. He'd missed his chance.

"Never mind I'll force it open, when I come back from the pub." He said aloud.

The Gorgon's Head

An unmasked man appeared in the door entry of the Gorgon Pub. It was unusual because this man had identified Angus's track suit well before he should have been able to see it. That was because he was actually AI. He was an East End London doorman part cloned into artificial intelligence along with current programmes and trends reserved to fool the masses. He was wearing the customary security jacket and black boots, denominating him as an AI security operative. By this time Angus knew he'd made a huge mistake. "God help me, na' wonder it's called the Gorgon's Head," he mumbled under his breath.

"Hibee supporter yer' a long way from home." The AI said recognising Angus's team colours laughing like a cockney costermonger.

Angus could see the man's security label. "Hell fire it's one of them' robot humans," he mumbled under his breath as the robot approached him.

"Danna' get too close Laddie, I'll put tha' head on ya', 'am just trying to get a few pints before I've got to go on a holiday." Even though Angus had whispered the words, the AI had registered Angus saying 'God help me' under his breath. Its plastic skin wrinkled with 'make believe' thought.

"Now that's something we don't like to hear. Never say God. I am not fully human so God is not welcome. That notion is anti-demoncratic." Angus couldn't help saying under his breath, "I'll feckin chin ya' stood there like a politically correct mannequin."

Angus knew the new word, demoncratic meant that the demon rulers were taking over everything enabled by New Babylonians. "Och' then ya' don't like the name God? What are ya' Laddie, some kind of Satanist?" Angus asserted. It took a moment for the information to sink into the AI operative. To all intents and purposes it was impossible to tell him apart from a normal human being. The bot had even got a small tattoo of the Fulham logo on its neck. The AI humans were not subject to being marked with the number of the beast like sovereign humans as they'd been programmed to be subservient to the New Babylonians as a matter of course.

There were four levels or castes of social order in the world now. The orchestrators had so far not been seen, and they were the Demons. Below them came the New Babylonian rulers and below them was the AI part human part technology and below them came the slave caste of marked humans. Those humans unmarked, which made up at least fifty percent of the population of the planet had no status and were considered outlaws. They were thus denominated in the end as Sovereign Outlaws. In these times it was illegal to have any kind of spiritual affiliation and the secular law cracked down on those who defied it. The phenomenon was labelled 'Science is better than God' by most of the media.

'The Four levels of New World Order'

1. Demons

2. New Babylonians

3. AI - Artificial Intelligence

4. Slave caste of marked humans denoted by masks and safety overalls

"I heard you ask God for help as well." The AI muttered.

"Aye what about it man. But ya' ken? Ya' not even a human ya' nowt but a vehicle for a once living person ya' a dead man. Danna' confuse yasel' wi' a sovereign human."

"A little tip for you, it is now illegal to mention or refer to God. Human beings are just hackable entities and there's nothing your God can do to help you."

"Aye that was uttered by some blackguard scientist …na' one believes him though, he's just bitter and twisted."

Angus gulped. "This poison goes way deeper into the heart of humanity."

The AI screwed its face up again with an inappropriate look of glee. It had registered his comment with those controlling the infernal Saturn computer under the Earth and Angus knew it.

Angus pushed through the pub doors engraved with the name of the brewery. It wasn't going to stop him getting a few beers and a couple of nips though, he thought with misguided bravado.

Inside it was like an East End type London pub from 1978. There was a collection of gangsters stood around the bar, clearly it was their manor. Some wore 1960's Italian suits fashionable amongst gangster types then with shiny leather shoes. The elegant cut of their suits was lost on these burley men used to intimidating others. Some had silk handkerchiefs in their top jacket pockets or other little touches like braided finery denominating them as classy thugs. But like the Gorgon pub doorman they too were Artificial Intelligence. Nearer to Angus stood the football supporters in their Fulham colours. The doorman

54

tapped Angus on the back, "Look mush you might wanna' keep away from dem' boys they'll fuckin' have ya'."

"Aye true, I am certainly not dressed for the occasion." Angus replied with a sense of irony looking down at his Hibernian tracksuit, knowing it could kick off trouble. The Fulham supporters were also AI bots but it would take a little time for them to register a Scottish side's colours in the centre of London. In fact, everything in the pub, even the pub dog was Artificial Intelligence. Flat nosed, the bulldog skittered about looking for fake crisps. In many real places living humans were being displaced by robots. There was no way of telling them apart, especially the latest models. They were complete with real blood and skin from the organ reclamation plants, run by what remained of the National Health Service. Its new name was 'World Global Health'.

As the world depopulation agenda swept full on, many people were going into hospital and just not coming out. In fact, Angela's mother had been one such victim. That's why she was doing as much as she could to help Angus now. She, like many others understood what was occurring but had been frozen by fear of the situation. She knew that in some supernatural way he was the key to the reversal of what had been happening.

Angus moved to the bar watched by all and the bots. The fake landlord now came over dressed in clothing from the Victorian period, long apron, bowler hat, big sideboards known as Dundrearies. Except the technical editors who had configured his AI characteristics had forgot to provide the relevant footwear. Instead, the Victorian London pub landlord wore modern designer trainers.

"Hello Sir, what can I get you, what'll it be? He asked, eyeing Angus's rucksack with the Grail in it.

55

"Aye Laddie they messed up ya' costume somewhere along the line; ya' about 120 years outta' date. And yet ya' trainers are monstrously modern." The landlord's face wrinkled calculating Angus's words. "I am sorry Sir I have no knowledge of 'Victorian costume', I will consult the handlers."

"I'll have a drink ya' ken', I'll ha' a pint of lager and a nip."

"I am sorry Sir what's a nip?" But then the landlord carried out mental calculations as he linked into the worldwide web. Indeed, it was a link that every human being left alive would be forced to connect to.

"Angus was running out of patience. "A nip is a double whisky no' an English measure ya' ken' I want the full Scottish measure of whisky. Johnnie Walker if you've got it. It's ma' brew."

The AI understood the command moving with indescribable speed and before Angus had looked up, the drinks were on the bar in front of him.

"For the mother of God, where the hell did tha' cam' from?"

There was a bill marked 'void' left next to drinks along with a packet of nuts. And the Victorian Landlord was away to serve someone else. Angus was anxious now realising he'd entered a theme park of an old London pub where all the AI inside had been conjured up from different times in modern history. He realised that the Fulham supporters were dressed as if from the late 90's. He remembered back to bleak Sunday afternoons up in Scotland watching footy in the bars of Leith. Angus took a large sup from his pint of lager and followed it up with a swig of the nip and the preferred drink combination of the proper Scotsman. Then everyone looked at Angus. It was just a brief co-ordinated glance which they did together. There were some London ladies sat together drinking 'rum and peps' in dresses from 1967, smoking fake cigarettes as well, looking over at Angus. Then they just stopped looking, carrying on with their soulless pastiche words copied from the lives of other people, recorded from old television documentaries assimilated and uploaded into the bots. Of course, Angus was aware about the progress with AI but he'd no idea that they'd started to replace real humans. And then he realised the bots had not been looking at him, but had been looking at his rucksack. Every one of them fixed a deadly stare at his rucksack where the Grail was. It was time to get the hell out of it. Angus supped his drinks quickly. Just as he'd finished the Victorian Pub Landlord skidded over in his apron with another round of a lager and nip. "That's on the house Sir no charge today it's from the owners." Angus looked over towards the gangsters and they nodded at him insolently. The AI doorman suddenly stood by the door intentionally blocking it. Angus looked at the nip.

"I hope this is a Scottish measure Laddie?" Angus was full of bravado.

"It is Sir, just as you like it. Please enjoy. By the way, the gentleman over there would like a word with you. I'll transfer your beverages."

Angus tightened the rucksack to his back and before he'd had time to object about his beverage being taken over to the gangsters it had already been placed next to their bottles of champagne. Angus walked over reluctantly near where a skinny pole dancer was just emerging to do the panther walk around her pole. Angus felt sick, to all intent and purposes the pole dancer was Angela McBride. Apart from the fact she'd got a tattoo which Angela would never have had. Sometimes the AI planners got their details wrong. Angus knew at that moment he was being set up.

The Italian suited gang boss adjusted his glasses. "Welcome to the Gorgon's Head Angus. Better in here with us than in the House of Commons me' ol' cock sparra. And look at the arse on that dancer." Angus felt the red mist of anger. The AI planners had orchestrated the situation and created a robot which looked like his dear friend Angela. How did they know he would do the wrong thing and come into the pub? What mechanism of prediction had they got?

Now they were using his memory of Angela to anger him. Somehow, they'd stolen the images of her from her mobile phone. The Angela bot gyrated twirling round the pole watched by the Fulham supporters who were leering and attempting to touch her. "Keep ya' grubby paws off her ya' bastards," Angus said realising he was being played.

"What are your plans, Angus?"

Angus winced inside. "Aye whisht' 'am just having a look around before I go on ma' holiday shall we say and how do you know my name?" Angus stood head and shoulders above the gangster group. He was weighing them up just in case of trouble. The Fulham supporters had stopped rabble rousing and stood gawping at the Angela bot doing the aeroplane spinning round the pole with her arm out. The hooligans jeered and made threatening comments as they would have done before the Acts of Sensibility had been made law designed to draw attention away from the real crimes against humanity.

"Let's have a look in ya' rucksack." The AI London gangsters were 'tooled up' with weapons which Angus had seen, bulging from their back pockets. 'Maybe they could see in the rucksack somehow?' Angus suspected. Or were they just acting on some kind of programmed evil instinct? Suddenly Angus felt vulnerable. He'd miscalculated the situation. For this had been engineered by the priests of the supercomputer called Saturn which was now known to be sentient. Curiously it was aware of itself as a living being. But there was more to it all which wasn't even known by those who had created it.

"Aye its nowt' ya' ken' it's just an old stonemason's drinking bowl he said remembering Andrew's words on the film of him discovering it." But of course, it was much more than that.

Angus' legs started to wobble. He grasped the nip glass with the whisky and downed it in one.

Another gangster chipped into the chat. "Good effort mush, a real man takes his whisky and in his Scottish team colours. Like it mate, fuck I like it, eh' Harry get him another one." The robot's detail was incredible. It had even got a gold tooth. And as if by magic another whisky nip appeared on the bar like a victualler's apparition whilst the Angela AI robot twirled on her pole.

With whisky starting to coarse through his veins, Angus was beginning to wake up to the danger. The waters of life were waking him up. He reached for the nip glass, simultaneously another of the gangster group grabbed his wrist and began to squeeze it with indescribable strength. Angus said nothing realising that the next few seconds would be critical to his survival. This was the AI's advantage but Angus's antidote to this was innovation. A thought like a thunderbolt came and he suddenly remembered back to his battles with the earlier versions of their kind back in the Calbunco volcanic crater in Chile. The whisky was loosening his thoughts and past recollections. With all his strength he pushed his hand under the AI's chin shoving it backwards whilst opening its clunky mouth. The AI staggered on it gyroscopic balance system. Simultaneously Angus grabbed the pint of lager and poured the pint down the robot's gullet. The thermal shock caused it to release its grip and Angus went into full fight mode. He watched its eyes revolve in its head like frantic ball bearings causing it to lose balance. It fell to the floor, legs flailing, and face nutting the ground. It was a situation that the other AI gangster had not been programmed to anticipate. They stood around chatting in gangster speak, whilst gangster bot 3 flailed around uncontrollably on the wooden boards of the Gorgon's Head pub.

"Yeah, let's have a look at what you got in the bag ya' Hibernian heretic and the downed robot began to sing the Hibernian anthem, 'Sunshine in Leith', from the floor." Malfunctioning, real blood dripped out of its ear pooling red on the boards whilst it sang songs from the floorboards from the East End of London like an insane Dick Van Dyke. "Knees up muvver' Brown, knees up muvver' Brown. Maybe it's because I'm a Londoner, that I love London town."

Angus got into full swing. He smacked gangster number 2 next to the bar so hard its eyeball popped out of its silicone fleshed head. The others came to grab him. Angus ducked down on the floor and crawled towards the door. Curiously the AI heat sensors lost connection to him. He was able to scurry along the boards as far the AI security door operative's black boots. Looking up from the floor Angus could see the pub landlord walking over from behind the bar with a shotgun. The Fulham supporters hit the deck holding their heads protectively like there was a London blitz bombing raid happening. Instead of backing down, Angus waited till he'd come out and was within his grasp to grab his legs. He would carry out a 'take down' dump and follow by a chest slam on it, with the intention of damaging its heart pump circuitry. From the floor Angus bounced up and levered all his weight in the form of a rugby tackle bang into the AI's legs. The pub landlord went over like a sack of coal being thrown off the back of a waggon. Angus smashed down onto him squashing his chest causing the Landlord's fingers to bend backwards as far as its wrist like they were made of rubber. Angus had succeeded in scrambling it. But then the shotgun went off from the ground sending shot spraying over the gangsters by mistake. Angus crawled for the pub door.

"Och, I canna believe this shite."

The London ladies began singing "Roll out the barrel, roll out of the barrel, Watney's Red Barrel tonight." with a dispossessed joy to the unfolding violence. They sang on with gusto just like the late 1960's London pub documentary they'd been contrived from. Gangsters appeared out of the smoke with their fake silicon skin blown off their faces, exposing high tech hardware with bulging white eyeballs and the familiar dark coloured pupils seen on all the AI hybrid human models. Within them though, were the real organs harvested from humans sent to the end of life terminals, cynically named Heaven's Highway Incorporated. It was where all those who were ill were sent for termination after the collapse of the old ways.

Angus knew the Grail bowl was safe in the rucksack on his back as he crawled for the door. It resonated like the gentle buzz of a bee. Okay, so he'd had a nasty shock, he'd made a mess of the portal moment and realised he must get back into the Temple. Just then the pub door was kicked in. All the torn-up AI characters and mayhem stopped dead.

The concierge from Andrew Sinclair's apartment stood there like a superhero. "Thank God man, I am sorry I did na' know." The concierge began to drag Angus along the wooden floorboards towards the exit. He was much stronger than he looked.

"No time to talk, I've disabled the Bots and you've got 5 minutes to get through the portal in the Temple." The concierge sighed deeply adding caustically, "I should have waited, I was told you would do something like this. But hell, you won't make me look bad you stupid man."

Angus got up from the floor bleeding from a new scar on his cheek. "Get moving Angus, I can't tell you how important it is. I'll finish off here. Go back through the door at the Temple now!"

Angus stumbled out onto the street from the Gorgon's Head. He looked back to see windows going through and glass exploding on to the street. The figure of the Concierge was karate chopping and gesticulating amongst the robots that remained standing. Boom! There was flash, bangs and more smoke accompanied by the sounds of crunching hardware. The concierge moved like a mad scything machine through the bots.

Successful Entry at the Temple Portal

Angus limped up the path to the door at the Temple, pushing through it. It clicked shut behind him with a resounding echo. He stood there in the silence shocked and dazed. He walked over to the stone effigy which looked like him. This time he recognised himself in its features. He walked past the other effigies of the Templars laid out in beautiful symbolic contortions upon the stone flags. He began to imagine them talking to him. But maybe there was some truth in that. The knight known as the Richardson Knight opened its shut stone eyes and began to talk gripping its carved sword. "Brave Knight do thy duty, do not let us down or you will receive more scars upon your soul." Sir Richardson's head cracked crunching back into position.

"Sure, I will do my duty. I canna' understand ya' posh tones Sir Knight. But och' right enough though, I know you from distant battles."

"Do your duty for the knights, the world needs you more than ever Sir Angus MacWilliam," said Sir William Marshal straightening from his contorted war pose from the floor of the Temple. The other knights' effigies sat up creaking and cracking in their stone armour as puffs of stone cracked and dust lifted into the air.

Angus touched the new scar on his own right cheek which had stopped bleeding. It had depth and would probably remain permanently like an old Heidelberg duelling scar reminding him of his wilful stupidity. The Heidelburg sword fencers were always marked with scars of initiation and proud of them. Curiously the stone effigy of himself now bore the same scar. It just appeared on the right cheek of the Angus effigy with stone dust rising into the air highlighted in a sunbeam. The scar carved itself before his eyes. Angus looked at the praying hands of the reclining statue of himself. Its hands were open like it should be holding something perfectly round. Time was running out, instinctively he took out the Grail bowl from the rucksack. It was still vibrating with a low bee like hum. Angus knew that the Grail bowl must be plugged into its exact reverse shape presented by his effigy's praying hands. He'd taken his allotted thirty seconds to experience the peace of his situation in the Temple. The beam of sunlight dropping through the Octagonal domed roof illuminating the other Templar effigies all laid out and contorted in battle positions supported by ornately crafted griffins and hunting dogs wrapped round their feet. Two doves sat on a stone ledge nudging each other. He moved forward and placed the Grail between the praying hands of his own effigy. The Grail turned and clicked into position like an isotope from a nuclear reactor. Now Angus could see his own effigy being carved in some other time quadrant. It was carving itself. It was warm there where a volcano smoked in the background above the floodwaters. Then all started to swirl around in a vortex sea whirlpool, a medieval Wurlitzer of merging time zones. All that Angus had forgotten he started to remember again including his battles with the early versions of the AI in Chile. He saw his wife from the Castello in Spain and watched their last Milonga Tango dance in Rosslyn Chapel's crypt. He saw the City of Light and the flights of falcons attacking the New Babylonian drones. He saw the horrible scorpion-tailed giant locusts, which had stung to death the New Babylonians in their tracks, killing them in that other place called Chile. The atmosphere was red like the ghostly transparent energy of life blood through its spiritual power. Angus swirled around in the vortex whirlpool of energy which had been blasted away to become a portal by the Holy Ark of the Covenant. He could smell that spice and dead flesh smell again of the Pirate

Brethren. He listened to the shouts of the Templars trying to save their vessels, as they flowed down into the underground realm on the way to Antarctica, to escape the deluge God had cast down on the Earth. He looked up to see the London Temple, the HQ of the Templars where his effigy had been placed, now full to the brim with blood. Then he felt the warm wet of the sea spraying onto him from the decks of the knight's war vessel, Pegasus. At last, he was back in that other world.

The Journey Continues to the Ice Tunnels under Antarctica

"Avast ye pirates save the vessels, furl the sails, and turn on the power!" The Pegasus wallowed in the trough of a huge wave; a wave flushing broken bits from enemy wreckage screeching along the steel bulwarks of Pegasus. Down below many of their war horses skittered and whinnied with confusion. As the Templars stabled a great number of horses in the vaults of the Temple of Solomon so it was the same for the stables in Pegasus.

"Angus where did you go? Help the wheelsman we need more men on the helm, we cannot afford to lose this ship, we carry the Holy Ark." Just as Angus lumbered over, the Templar Master added, "By the way that new scar you've got for yourself will remind you of the peril the world is in next time you get distracted, shall we say. That's all I am saying." Angus had heard the statement 'that's all I am saying' many times from Andrew Sinclair. But where was he now? If he wasn't in the previous world he must be here somewhere.

Back on the helm deck, three of the Pirate Brethren were wrestling with the Pegasus's wheel trying to keep her steady. Angus lumbered over putting his shoulder behind it. Suddenly a huge wave engulfed the Pegasus but she remained under control in the seething vortex of swirling sea. As expected, Pegasus's ether power units jolted and kicked in and she began to surf with the swirl. Her engines had been created by none other than Nikola Tesla himself, working on the principle of tapping the natural energy which surrounded the Earth as a viable power source. There was no belching smoke here, just unrestrained steady throbbing power. Tesla and many other of the avant-garde Earth influencers like Admiral Byrd had at some point been to where the Pegasus and the vessels of the pirates and knights were going. Sailing to a place where God's enemies had also gone and where others of their kind remained. From these underground places it was known they carried out abysmal rituals against the Earth and God and the sanctity of blood.

All their vessels had made it through the deluge following the Pegasus like nautical outriders. The Templar Admiral of the Pegasus encouraged Angus and the pirate helmsman who were fighting with the ship's wheel. "Steady as she goes brothers, keep her steady!" Her decks were seething with both knights and pirates going about their duties, carrying out their various sea tasks, stowing ropes away, preparing for what was to come. Pegasus's Templar Admiral pushed up the stairs onto the helm.

"Angus give me the Grail; I'll put it somewhere safe until this is over."

"Aye it's burning a hole in time itself!"

Angus handed it over knowing it would be safe for it was the key to entering both worlds. Right away some Knights of Saint John came over to assist him back down the stairs. Laura Bellamy was standing by ready to lend a hand if the wheelsman needed it. Pegasus was surfing the safer seas towards a huge chasm-opening, worn smooth by raging surf as wide as London Bridge, where Angus had kept safe as part of his penance, but a penance designed to protect him.

The Light Bearers

There was a cowled lady holding a lantern high above the rocks; some of the Templars had come out from below decks waving lanterns at the figure. "Who the hell is that?" Angus cried out amazed that another living being was also in this land.

"Don't ask now! Just keep your mind on keeping us on course through the gorge."

Angus bit his lip keeping his mouth shut. He'd been getting into too much trouble as it was, it was time to focus. He put his shoulder into the ship's wheel juddering with strain.

"They are the early Light Bearers. There's not many of them remaining down here." Another burst of waves rolled over the Pegasus's decks. You will get to meet them very soon. They are preparing for our fleet in the harbour built by the pre-Atlanteans." Pegasus surged on through the sea dipping down into a trough and rising on a wave.

Angus felt a wash of melancholy about the figure he'd seen on the chasm tops with the light. She reminded him of someone. There was the faint recollection of fragmented love like a flickering jigsaw puzzle with pieces missing. He concentrated on fighting to keep the Pegasus on course with the pirates. The sickly smell of death and spices was overwhelming whenever they were near as his memory of his time in London grew distant. Only the effigy image of himself in his mind's eye was clear like it was a reminder of the way back. For his existence traversed several layers of time which scientists had named dimensions, only he had no desire to return to that world of New

Babylon centred in London. It was a world where humanity had abandoned God and welcomed in a supercomputer called Saturn. This monster would regulate them so that they would never have to think for themselves again. It would decide who would live and die according to the New Babylonian edicts of world control. And if a person happened to be seriously ill they were simply brought into the end of life terminals to be humanely dispatched, their good organs and body parts recycled through the AI factories. Had Angus known the full extent of the nature of people in the Gorgon's Head he would have kept away, for they were hybrid human Artificial Intelligence, cobbled back together after being humanely killed. Blood and microchips were unnaturally synthesised creating a controllable soulless being. Just then the Templar Admiral turned to Angus. "It's alright Angus if we succeed down here where God has sent us, he will take care of the Saturn Supercomputer and its worshipers."

"Och' man how did ya' know what I was thinking?"

Angus looked aft and saw that many of the other vessels were catching up. All the Templar ships had made it through the vortex and for that he said a quiet prayer of thanks to God. Then the light he'd seen on the tops flickered up forward of Pegasus as she rounded the chasm entrance. Graciously they encountered a calm sea in the great basin, which diminished rapidly to millpond flat as the supernatural vortex ceased giving way to stillness. More vessels followed them into the black waters. The crews stood back relieved that their voyage of descent into the tunnels beneath Antarctica was drawing to completion.

"Thank God man, I thought we were doomed."

"Not quite, Angus not quite," replied the Templar Scientist.

69

The Light Bearers had done their job. Angus looked up gratefully with praying hands to heaven. Then he helped tie up all the other vessels with a crew of pirates. De Molay had ordered they make ready their forces for the arduous march to the ice realms under Antarctica to confront the great demon army in its entirety. But for now, the great Host of God was at liberty to rest and prepare. At last Andrew Sinclair appeared. He came from the aft cabin where Templar dignitaries were assigned to some comfort despite the incredible storm they'd come through. Reiner Gorst who had written a description of his capture by the pirates back in the swamps of Chiloe in UB96 in 1945 was with them but severely compromised in his wheelchair. Reiner's mind was still clear and functioning. He had managed to extract important information from several special captured SS Officers about the nature of German explorations in Antarctica and what their forces had been attempting to do before they died of old age, all bar one. Reiner had made a huge report as part of his reparation to the world and God, he was not expected to make it back from the tunnels. Soon Reiner would be taken to the Nazi base from where the demon army had been summoned by Nazi occult scientists aligned with the New Babylonians. Their orders had come from Hitler himself through the occult Thule Society. The Templars had prolonged Reiner's life to be able to get them to the Nazi base where the secret which had been kept from the world resided.

Andrew in his Templar Priest's mantle and cap came out of the dignitaries' cabin scowling at Reiner Gorst after listening to his report. "Ah Angus you're back. Looks like you missed the worst of the storm. And what's that, a nice scar of reckoning by the looks of it. I'd heard you've had some adventures whilst you've been away. But then you needed to experience what's going on in the real world. It's all pretty grim isn't it? Be content you are part way to helping us defeat it."

"I thought God had destroyed the other world Andrew?" Angus pleaded.

"It's deep Angus, very deep. But there's more than one world, more than one world. I sent a good chap to help you. I sent Smithers the concierge at my apartment down on the Thames. A trusted warrior and a long time ago he was my squire. He was promoted after several battles against the New Babylonians and he knew you were returning. And as you will learn, he fought against the Old Babylonians."

"Och' man thanks for that and by Christ he can fight. He destroyed all the AI in the Gorgon's Head, there was blood and microchips all over the pub."

Andrew grinned. "Yes, Smithers would do that quite easily, a damn fine fighting man if ever there was one."

Steadily the Pegasus entered the natural cliff harbour prepared for them. The other vessels and launches waited their turn in the basin rocking gently in the last of the swell caused by the vortex. Yet outside the entrance to the harbour basin the vortex raged past it. Pegasus led the way and soon the pirates were tying her up in her mooring. All the crew disembarked onto the natural harbour carved out by the last race of Atlantis. Angus was surprised at how many warriors came out of the ships. They had all come from their City of Light above, preparing to go deeper down the tunnels to Antarctica. Yet soon the deluge God had sent would start to pull back the waters and the survivors could start to rebuild their lives. Above them God had sent the deluge to regulate the wickedness of mankind once again and to destroy their evil of cobbling together of men and machines. Microchipped blood and flesh failed. These Dr Moreau type human hybrids existed contrary to the law of God and had, nevertheless, been soundly beaten by the low-tech approach of the knights and pirates. One by one the vessels of the Host of God berthed and were tied up against the harbour wall and purpose-built silos. Now they could rest a while before their great march into the underworld.

Then the first of the Light Bearers appeared out of nowhere. It was the lady with the lamp Angus had seen up on the canyon tops who had pinged his recognition of her somehow.

"Welcome knights and pirates you are here on the outer reaches of the tunnels," said the Light Bearer.

Angus knew she had a Spanish accent different from say, Bolivian or Argentinean Spanish. She looked over at him without any hint of recognising him though. Once she had been his wife in the medieval period at Seville, Spain. And then he remembered how they were together before the deluge in Chile. He knew she had owned a small island situated in Chiloe, called the Island of Sailing Souls. He knew that once she had brought him to the City of Light and that her name had been Vanessa Bermodes. But he was having difficulty getting any further than that. In fact, he sat down feeling disorientated by the situation. Andrew Sinclair came over with a vial of smelling salts.

"Here take these, they'll stop the feeling."

"Och' cheers' Andrew by Christ I need them," Angus replied snorting deeply at the bottle.

Another battalion of hooded female Light Bearers arrived to illuminate the dockside to make it easier for the pirates and knights to prepare for their intrepid march. It appeared that who Angus had once known as Vanessa Bermodes was in charge of the other Light Bearers.

All of them had closed eyes for the Light Bearers were blind, blind to the Light they brought to others.

"Not to worry Angus these Light Bearers have remarkable gifts of prophecy and they can turn themselves into any version of humanity at will where they can see just like them." Andrew said. "But here they are blind. They've always been here and always will be."

Angus didn't know what to say, he also knew that sentimentality would not be good for him here. He got up and started to help the others coming out of the vessels.

"Good man Angus, it's the only way to deal with it. Be brave and help others."

Angus couldn't help himself. He waited till Andrew had gone and walked over to the Light Bearers' Leader. She was aware of him and who he was as the Grail Knight but nothing more.

"Stay back good knight, your place is not here, be with your own kind." The Lady Light Bearer stood solemnly silent. But somehow the words had entered Angus's mind spoken clearly, transparently telepathic. Angus held out his hand. "Again knight, go to your tasks. For you are not known here with us," she said. The other Light Bearers floated over in their white cloaks and formed a protective circle around her. He listened to their words in his mind, their chattering saying the same things.

"He thinks she is his wife; he dares to think she is his. He cannot understand time and what we do, what we are. Look now, his Lord comes for him, he knows we cannot be fathomed, he knows now to leave us be." "Angus bloody hell, I've explained some things which cannot be comprehended here, leave them alone they do not want you near them!"

"Good he will go now to his duty, he will go now." And together they sang a lament in some ghostly unknown language as Angus backed away with watery eyes unable to understand the state of affairs.

"Ya canna' beat a bit of rejection Andrew Lad, to get ya' focus back." He looked back to see the cohort of Light Bearers moving back as if one, from where they had come.

"The thing is Angus the woman you thought was your wife was actually playing the role, you've been played like a chess piece in this huge game that's going on between good and evil. Be thankful you also have a role to play just like us all."

"But what about Chile and the Island where I stayed at the Hacienda in Santiago, Vanessa Bermodes and Don Carlos the Milonga Tango dancer?"

Andrew said nothing, Angus had more respect for Andrew than anybody else, but he was getting angry at the thoughts of the situation as if he were an unwilling player in some unreal video game.

"Och Andrew, faking into the role eh? she did a great job Laddie."

"Always back to your pride Angus, but I suppose this whole situation is a learning curve for you?" Andrew smiled knowingly. "I'd get some rest, there's a 'gathering Conclave' first thing in the morning. Go to your accommodation over there."

Admiral Byrd, Knight Grand Cross

Andrew pointed over at the stout wooden doors in the mountain side.

"You'll be pleased to know that Admiral Byrd was the last person to have occupied the butterfly room. More about him later though, when you will find out he was once a knight also."

Angus knew all about the adventuring US Navy Admiral, apparently chased away from his great discovery by aliens in their super spacecraft. There had been speculation about the collusion between the so-called aliens and a breakaway faction of Nazis. That had been the case until something terrible had occurred which was described as 'an attack of demons and fallen angels' who had hidden themselves under Antarctica. Only Admiral Byrd knew the truth, but he'd signed a pact of silence with his own government. Still, there was an altar of arrangements on Byrd's desk under a mirror. What could this be?

Angus walked slowly over to it. All around thousands of butterflies were rising and falling on their papery wings, fluttering in that up and down way which identified them as messengers of God and bearers of goodwill from dead relatives. They followed Angus like an ethereal bodyguard to the door of his room carved out of the mountain. He walked in holding the rucksack with the Grail, the ring, and his gold. He entered leaving the door open collapsing and slumping on the bed trying to stave off sleep. Yet the door which he'd left open was drawn closed by the formation of butterflies covering it, wafting their wings gently until it shut.

Above the desk on the altar in the room was a portrait of Admiral Byrd, the man who had ventured to find the truth in the tunnels. He smiled enigmatically, his eyes looking downwards onto the desk below. Angus looked to where Byrd's eyes were fixed on the desk from the picture. There was a book there with well-worn edges. On it was written *'The Journal of Admiral Byrd'*, in which he'd written about his exploration and the lost story of the inner Earth and what had been discovered. Above the desk there was a small hole in the rock with a cork plug in it. Angus pulled it out and light streamed through from some outer source illuminating the desk and Journal. Although he felt he was being intrusive he opened it and began to read the words penned in longhand like the handwriting of William Shakespeare. It began with Byrd's wondrous dedication. There was a dull thud like an old radio being tuned and a hologram appeared of the enigmatic Admiral in his navy uniform. He flickered on and off seemingly making his address personally to Angus.

"I have seen wondrous things, beings and events, but I have also seen unspeakable evil here in the tunnels. Only the power of God can save us now. Down here I have also seen such beauty which would make any man stay out the rest of his life here in the name of God. But there are also things there that no man should see. There are monsters as well as men which you have never seen the likes of in your existence on the surface..."

Admiral Byrd Knight Grand Cross

Before Angus had any chance to read further there was a hard knock on the door. It was Andrew Sinclair. He opened it and marched in. "Angus you are not supposed to be looking at that Journal, there are things in it which may well upset you. Close it and get some sleep we have an arduous journey to get through. When you get there you'll realise that Admiral Byrd's Journal is only half the story."

"Och' aye Andrew you are such a spoiler sometimes!" he said closing the journal and watching Admiral Byrd's hologram fade away.

In the morning the butterflies had gone from the wooden door where Angus had slept and were now covering the whole chasm gorge and mountainside. Angus had been woken by the great trumpets of the Light Bearers meaning it was dawn. Outside, the knights were gathering their war gear as were the Pirate Brethren. They fed and armoured their horses. They mustered ready to begin marching into the tunnels.

The mounted Templar Knights totalled 450 alongside the same number of Knights of Saint John making 900 highly trained warriors both in spiritual matters and of the flesh of the fight. The Templar 'men at arms' along with the other foot soldiers gathered and lined up in square formation with their spears and shields like the phalanxes of Alexander the Great. They totalled 6,000 and all of them were trained foot soldiers. These soldiers were the stoic Sergeant at Arms who fought from the ground and occasionally on horseback supporting the knights. Next to them were the irregular Pirate Brethren who numbered 300 standing ready and carrying their cutlasses and pistols. But as their enemies would discover, their flintlock pistols were far more advanced than that. The supply baggage trains were almost ready to go. The wooden boxes holding their secret weapons were on the baggage trains. The Holy Ark had been guarded all the time by the Levi Priests and was about to be raised up.

Angus came out of his room in the rock to see his Templar Quester's mantle laid out ready and on it was the Grail bowl. His famous sword lay next to it along with his vest of mail. Angus automatically put them on and waited for Jacques de Molay to lead the expedition. He appeared but due to his great age and the tortures he'd recovered from was now sat on a small horseless chariot. It was harnessed to the unknown magnetic energy from the Earth propelled by the Schumann resonance. Behind him were the Templar Knights mounted on their war horses. Angus's mount was brought out to him snorting and hoofing the ground. Still Angus had insisted on wearing his Hibernian track suit and scarf. No one questioned it. De Molay the last Grand Master of the Templars hovered above the rest and began his stirring address to the host. He began, saying,

"I will bring you out of Egypt. I will rid you of their bondage. I will redeem you." Strained he looked around as if encumbered by the weight of his responsibilities. "All those gathered know the peril which awaits us. We know our sacred duty is our calling. Know that I will be with you till the end." There were murmurings of agreement from the army.

Finally, de Molay said, "we know the importance of this operation against the New Babylonians; this is an expedition to destroy their demonic power once and for all."

Everyone nodded, preparing for the march down the tunnels towards Antarctica. The baggage train packed with their extreme silk thermals and special weaponry was being organised by the Templar scientists. Boxes of intriguing species would be used against the demons and those that worked for them under Antarctica. The Templars and Pirate Brethren had their silk body armour designed with special antiseptic properties which would protect them from the poisonous bile of the mouths and fingernails of the infernal demon army.

"Now Angus MacWilliam, pass the Grail bowl in the customary way," the Templar Marshal shouted mounting his horse, "and make sure you wear the ring of Armageddon!"

Angus took the ring out of his rucksack putting it on the index finger of his right hand. Even in the gloomy dawn it did not shine; when the time was right though, it would shine illuminated by glory.

Automatically, Angus drank from the Grail bowl from the saddle of his horse. He passed it to the knight next to him. No one knew what the potion was in the bowl, only that it grounded each and every one of them enhancing their connection to God. They all began to sing the Psalm of King David for spiritual fortification for the journey. The Grail bowl was in turn passed round every man and women present yet when it came back it was still full of the amber liquid. When the ritual had finished the amber liquid turned into a swarm of bees, buzzing away up the side of the gorge.

De Molay gave the order to march into the tunnels which waited, opening like the great mouth of a monster under the mountain. The army of knights and pirates marched slowly through the gaping maw.

Jacques de Molay hovered upwards. "Bring out the Holy Ark of God!" Andrew Sinclair led a contingent of seven purple robed High Priests from the rear. These were Levi Priests from the house of Aaron, the brother of Moses.

The Army of God rested now under the area called Patagonia, a place where renegades and those fleeing from the status quo above often went. The waters had started to abate and mountain tops were pushing through resembling a multitude of Islands now that the surface deluge was abating.

The March to Fight the Great Demon Army

"We march to the war, God is with us," de Molay cried from his hover chariot in the giant tunnel. Above, on the mountain the Light Bearers came with their lanterns, as if illuminating the courage of knights and pirates. The host of warriors looked up silently marching into the tunnel behind their Grand Master. As they went, the High Priests bearing the Holy Ark, moved through their ranks and strode to the front where the Templars marched and where darkness came to cover them.

Andrew Sinclair, also robed in purple cried out, "Start the Holy Ark! We need the Light of God here so that we can see our enemy!"

De Molay nodded his head with satisfaction. As the Holy Light from the Ark began to illuminate all around them, so the Light Bearers started to pull back from the army having done their job. The army entered the tunnels illuminated by the Ark as their shadows danced like giants on the tunnel walls. Now all could see the carvings and symbols from a previous, more enlightened race. There were hundreds of images of exotic insects from the inacus wasp to giant locusts with their stinging scorpion tails further developed by the Templar scientists to fight the New Babylonians. There were also sea life varieties from conger eels to manta stingrays and other monstrous entities known to have existed in the dark ages of humanity. Further in, there were also examples of predators carved from panthers and lions to tigers and pumas and other living things, except they had wings and sometimes twin heads.

Then the Holy Light from the Ark illuminated carvings of beings riding on the backs of giant ants. What mighty civilisation had carved such a spectacle? And more importantly where had they gone?

From his hover chariot de Molay brought out a navigation aid and began turning its bronze dials. The instrument had been adapted to work under the ice and to get them through the first quadrant of ice tunnels. The further they went towards Antarctica the colder they thought it would become. But they'd made an early miscalculation as in fact the ice in the tunnels diminished. The tunnels began to tighten. There was a smell of fresh vegetation and the Templar horses began to scent the clean water. Light shone in the larger space where they were heading as their war horses whinnied with expectation.

De Molay's hover chariot drifted down to the army below which parted in a circle around him. Andrew Sinclair and the Levi Priests always held back from the main body of the army due to the invincible power of the Ark.

De Molay spoke, "Army of God I have news for you. There will be a chance to rest in fourteen leagues into the tunnels of the pre-Atlanteans. We will be met by guides and friends. We march on."

They marched on as steam lifted like smoke from them as testimony to their exertions. Their forward ranks had now organised themselves into a V formation led by their officers. The daughter of the famous pirate Sam Bellamy, Laura Bellamy stood with them in her capacity as Master of the Pirate Brethren. She was assisted by two pirate captains. De Molay hovered in and out of the host inspiring them to march to the inevitable war ahead. The host surged on away from the cold tunnels, thousands of spears bristling. "Take your place with us now Angus, you've earned it," declared the Grand Master of the

Knights of Saint John. Angus spurred his mount forward to join the vanguard knights. He held the handle of his great sword as his horse skittered forward in anticipation.

Laura Bellamy looked at Angus from her stout war horse. "It won't be long brother before we are fighting in the front lines together," she said, brandishing her cutlass.

"Aye Lass I am ready, I am ready!" Angus said.

She'd witnessed Angus fight in the test pit and triumph against one of her Pirate Brethren who had suffered at his hand for accusing him of being a coward. The fight had taken place under their articles of combat in the pit. Much of those memories were returning now Angus was back at the source. The Grand Master made sure the Holy Ark was following the train of knights and pirates. Sure enough Andrew Sinclair raised his hand from below, acknowledging the Grand Master leading them to an opening by a clear running river. Most of the ice had disappeared. The host followed de Molay into the clearing where the water was pure enough to drink.

"Replenish and fill the water canisters. The water is good here and will refresh body and soul," de Molay ordered.

De Molay disappeared temporarily from sight in the shadow of the waterfall. He was going to meet the pre-Atlanteans on their way as promised. He shouted back from the waterfall. "Steady your horses, steady them well! The ant riders are coming, dismount!"

The Ant Riders

At first it appeared like a phalanx of bending spears was getting nearer. But they were moving strangely like a field of wheat in the wind. The powerful waterfall acted as a curtain through which the approaching cohorts of pre-Atlanteans could not be seen. The Host of God dismounted and held their horses securely. These horses were disciplined and trained for war and would fight kicking out their strong legs and hooves at the enemy. The men and women at arms moved together as they'd been trained to do. The horses skittered forward on the frosty ground. Once they'd scented what was coming they calmed down even though it was terrible to behold. The trembling feelers of the giant ants appeared from behind the veil of the waterfall sensing the energies of the Host of God. The ants were larger than the war horses. Their huge jaws known as mandibles opened exposing a formidable array of razor teeth. All their six legs had been wrapped in chainmail and their heads helmeted like a steel bonnet. They pushed through the curtain of water as drips rolled off their bodies. Sat saddled behind the head of each ant was a woman, but with some natural modifications to allow her to survive under the Earth. Their eyes were cat-like to help with the darkness in the tunnels. Their hair was cropped for war and as white as de Molay's beard. Their bodies were efficiently muscled and their armour was a silken flowing garment which was cool in the heat or warm in the cold and spun from giant moth silk. They rode the ants with strength and skill using telepathy to urge them on. The Army of God drew breath, making the sound of the lower notes of a church organ, like a sound of controlled astonishment. In total one hundred riders had come up from under the tunnels. One by one they arranged themselves into a half-moon formation in front of the main Host of God. The Templar Scientist who had created them stepped forward. Angus knew him well from the locust pit he'd helped create in the City of Light and from whom he'd received deep insight, to help him win the day against the Artificial Intelligence above. It was time to address the host which was his duty. Instinctively the host pushed closer together ready to create a shield wall against a possible sneak attack.

"Be not afraid Host of God, they are here to help us. I should know I helped create them." De Molay said swooshing down to the ground.

Angus stepped forward compelled to say something. "Aye it's true I saw the scorpion-tailed giant locusts down in the pit whilst at the City of Light," he said looking up through the cavernous cave. "We can depend on them, believe me." Then he drew his Viking sword and raised it high. A cheer came out of the host. "You see, we kept pace with the advancement of the enemy down here. What you will encounter under the ice is like nothing you will ever see again. Be ready all of you for courage is your shield against them."

Angus held his sword high again. "Onward to fight the demons. God is with us."

The ant riders' cohort filed into line, the chainmail on their legs clinking gently. The ants sensed the mood vibration coming from the Host of God. Their leader urged her mount to kneel so that it knelt down on its front legs whilst watching the host carefully. The giant ant turned round and swivelled it's feelers so that they faced backwards enabling it's rider to grasp them to dismount. All the other ant riders drew closer to their leader. She walked over to Angus watched by her mount. All the time she moved gracefully across from the waterfall. She was still connected by her mind to the giant ant which remained kneeling in its interlocking armour. This special biomimetic armour mimicked that of the ironclad beetle which can withstand huge pressure. The Templar Scientist had designed the armour of the ants at the City of Light after studying the secret language of numbers inherent in all things.

At one point in their genesis, the ant riders had once been native Mapuche women whose families were connected to the forests above. They had formed alliances with pirates who had brought them to the Templars. They, like many indigenous peoples in the world, had been attacked and exploited by empire building European dynasties. Such evil families were the forerunners of the New Babylonians whom the Host of God had come to confront. Not just the physical army of men and machines but also the great demon army which backed every twisted move the New Babylonians made on the earth above. The ant riders had allowed themselves to be modified for life under their own country in order to serve the greater good. This entailed some modification from how they previously looked. For now, they had developed thicker skin and improved eyesight, enabling them to see without goggles in extreme temperatures. They appeared with narrow eye sockets and lids like those of chameleons with an inner lid membrane to protect against intense temperatures. But most of all they'd developed their sixth sense of communication through their minds. This instinct was always with the Mapuche from the beginning and they used telepathy as their main form of communication with each other. It was known to have helped them in the defence of their lands in Chile against the Incas of Peru. It was a special gift that the Templars had learned from the Mapuche natives. Their leader communicated to the Templar Scientist. The information she passed was not good news. The demon army had swelled in size with abominations and beasts from the deeper realms.

The Host of God drank and gathered more of the special water from the waterfall. De Molay gave the order to continue down the tunnels which grew dark again after the oasis. The Holy Ark, which Andrew Sinclair was assisting the Levi Priests with, was put into action and soon its light was illuminating the tunnels. No one knew what civilisation had created these tunnels and it was possible no one ever would. De Molay hovered forward slumped with exhaustion. "I have news from above. The deluge flooding is starting to abate and fall back. I am told that many have died and that a few have survived. The New Babylonians have retreated to their mountain fortresses and wait behind sealed steel doors to come out. Their plan is to emerge to massacre all the survivors on the planet summoning the demon army to assist them."

Angus MacWilliam could not keep quiet. "Aye but we will not let that happen Grand Master for we are here to end them now. And if we canna' do it in the world we came from then we will meet them in the other and finish it there!"

"That's the spirit Angus, but let me continue." he said adjusting himself in the cockpit into a more comfortable position. "Each warrior's courage down here increases tenfold under the law of God. Soon more good survivors will join us. And although they've adapted differently to those of us above, they remain with good soul."

Another great cheer lifted from the Host of God and they marched on. Ice appeared on the tunnel sides crystallising before their eyes like a stark warning not to continue marching. Although it was warm now something cold and lifeless was on its way.

The Battle in the Ice Tunnels

"Flesh and those things born of it exist in the frequency of the now. The things of the spirit exist in the realms around it and are still able to influence it. That is the way the power of prayer takes effect over flesh, from the inside out." Dr Andrew Sinclair put his hand on Angus's shoulder continuing. "This is where the demon army will manifest itself converting from vile spirit to rancid flesh."

Angus rested his sword in the 'on guard' position leaning it against his shoulder. The rest of the Army of God arranged itself into battle formation. Angus would need to be the first man into the fray. But Grand Master De Molay would lead them out. Sure enough the ice tunnels ahead began to freeze as spiralling rings of white ice crackled down towards them set in motion by the approaching demon army. Then green gasses from the hollow regions began to appear with the consistency of coffin liquor. It was a fearsome visceral brew from the fermenting flesh of the dead. It was the basest form of malignancy from where the demon army would rise. First to appear were the lower demons like pawns in a chess game. Hunched over and deformed they sprouted from the green gas taking root in the coffin liquor. De Molay saw them first and shouted down to the army below from his hover chariot. "Look they come! There! And over there! And yet another growing from the poison!" Demons sprouted in lines in front of them surmounted by ice all around. The strange thing was that although these lowly demons were immeasurably deformed their faces were those of recognisable media celebrities and politicians. For they wore the faces of those who read the news about the coming enslavement of humanity and the politicians who made the laws paid for by New Babylonians.

Angus's mind stretched back to his early life where he was at one with nature fishing in the Pentland Firth. He thought of the goodness of all the people he'd grown up with and how his family had nurtured him. Tears welled up in his eyes. He wiped them away with the back of his hand. Time stopped still for his tears, a microsecond of freeze-framed goodness like the pleading hands of praying Mary.

He reached for his war helm formed using natural engineering by which God had created the limpet and abalone shell, known to be the strongest geometric form on the planet. He put his helmet on in effect masking his grief for what had gone before as the lesser demons multiplied before the Army of God. The vile King of the Demons, Agrimas, was on his way with the rest of his stinking multitudes. He had already ascertained the strength of the Army of God, sending his lowliest demons to fill the space in front ranks of his army ready for the attack. From time to time their faces changed to those of media personalities and then back to the baseless faces of demons. They carried all kinds of weapons from high powered machine guns to various swords and lances. Down in the tunnels all weapons were equal but the strongest weapon of all was prayer. Following closely there would be an array of genetically modified animals and insects brought into the equation by both sides.

The battle in the ice tunnels had begun. The lower demons organised themselves in rough lines. First they released hybrid animals which went lumbering, skulking and lurching forward through the ranks of the lower demons who parted to let the monsters through. The Templars who had formed a vanguard in front of the Army of God prepared as de Molay deployed the ant riders waving his hand from his hover chariot above. Both flanks parted into two broad columns so that the ant riders could get through. The lead rider urged them forward and as he did so the giant ant lifted itself onto its four back legs giving the rider more height. They drove forward against the frenzied monsters snapping at them with their mandible jaws. The lower demons were inadequate in combat against the ant riders. Their only advantage was their numbers as more of their kind flooded in though the tunnels to the battle ground. The phalanx of ant riders stopped them in their tracks because their leg armour was invulnerable to the demons' swords. De Molay shook his head in disbelief when he saw thousands of the lower demons appearing from the pits of hell. Everyone knew that a well-formed charge by the Templar Host could inflict devastating damage on the lowly demon cohorts. At first, the hard work was left to the 200 ant riders now battling them. De Molay ordered the Templar charge to gather and prepare. The Templar Scientist was ordered forward walking behind a large cart with a huge glass box on it set between two poles like a catafalque. The box was full of giant locusts with their stinging scorpion tails. The locust host would seek out those with the damned blood. The Templar Scientist dropped his hand signalling for the boxes to be open. The glass fronted door was opened and a cloud of winged locusts flew up above the armies. Seeing this the ant riders spurred on their giant mounts and increased the killing of the terrible monsters. As the giant locusts dropped on them the Templar charge began. De Molay gave the enemy war on two fronts. As the battle raged all around Angus he began to feel strange. It is difficult to describe what he was feeling. Only that we must be reminded of how it might feel to die and to go through that feeling of wondering if anything was coming after it. He slumped down behind a stone and felt its roughness. It was the last bit of reality from that place but soon he would be in another.

Above Loch Eriboll

Angus lay there in the still sharp night. The stone slab on which he was crumpled was numbingly cold. Around him were stone blocks looking like guards of the old henge structure. The Wheelhouse above was where the Israelites had once plotted out their sacred calendar of feasts and it was illuminated in streaming light from the moon high above the plateau. The place was known by villagers who strayed up here from the villages below, for they gave accounts of having seen people dressed in the clothes from other ages. Angus could see some of them stood by the stones, their milky white faces looking at him. One gaunt old man looked over like a refugee from the Highland clearings. Yet behind him was a Viking from a thousand years earlier stood in his war helm. There were medieval women there too, watching and dressed in long Arthurian dresses. And a child played in a puddle with a boat.

"Och come on you people ya' better be here to help me!" Angus smiled unafraid of them knowing that in some other dimension they lived.

Night clouds passed overhead, their shadows darkening as they scudded across the fallen stone structure. He grasped instinctively for his sword, the 'head hewer' as he had called it after the battle in the ice cavern. It was not there, this time it was gone. God had removed it and now spoke through the whispers of the heather around him. "Go to Loch Eriboll and you will be met by a friend to find the demon slaying stone sword, the sword which lives in the water fashioned here in heaven from a meteorite." Angus struggled to his feet leaning on a nearby standing stone. "Och naw' I canna' go on with this I just canna', what more canna' do?"

Angus was not alone. A light breeze raked through the yellow gorse and purple heather around. He saw something slip behind a stone. And when he looked again there was something laying on a fallen stone meant for him. At first it looked like the collapsed shadow of a human. He walked over to the muddy ground still aching from the pains of battle whilst he had heavy thoughts of what was to come. His fingers grasped the skin of the gossamer fabric as light as air placed on stone as heavy as dark matter.

"Och' it's that angel skin stuff man! Nothing can touch me with this on ma' back." He took off his clothes and began to slide into the gold matrix fabric the colour of honey. The freezing temperatures were irrelevant now, nothing could defy the gossamer's capacity to insulate nor could any amount of rain wet him. He stood there under the moonlight watching the angel-skin glimmer. "Aye alright I'll put ma' clothes back on over it." As he did the flying entity which had delivered it scaled the standing stone. He could see its luminescent wings flick together as it vaulted away with green eyes penetrating the darkness. Angus had been attended by a Malakhim, a so called 'plain angel' of the ninth realm, sent to attend to the needs of living beings. The Malakhim had been assigned to Angus to watch his every move in dangerous circumstances. Angus stumbled in the mud onto his knees and to his surprise bounced back to his feet filled with new strength. "Alright man 'am on ma' way ye' 're the boss." He spoke to God like he was a publican in a bar. It was a journey not to be undertaken lightly even in the daytime and now the temperature had fallen further. Angus set off down the mountain away from the Wheelhouse portal. He'd thought in a negative moment that this place would be a good place to die in peace, nestled away in the heather, his soul ready to ascend to find the Light. He drifted back to his time on the mountain; back to when he'd witnessed four stags bolt and thunder away in the heather, near the makeshift monument to the sailors of HMS Hood further down. One visit was all it took to be bewitched above Loch Eriboll so close as it was to the veil between the living and the dead. Great slabs of granite twinkled in the moonlight below and were the only areas on his descent which was not heather and bracken. He had no recollection of how long he had been trailing down the mountain. Would it matter if he slept in peace for a while? He'd already seen the spot where he would take a rest in a place of natural safety. There was a place against the granite outcrop which appeared flattened amongst the dead bracken like a giant had slept there. It was close enough to the rock face to afford shelter to any weary soul, whether animal or human. He went over watching his footsteps on the steep slopes on a path where he walked like he'd trod there a million times. As the snow began to fall he dropped down onto his knees and gently slumped over. The wet snowflakes fell on his face, strangely warm and tingling as the bracken sprung back under him like a huge blanket. The temperature continued to drop yet Angus remained warm in the 'angel skin' under his real clothes. His heartbeat slowed whilst his breathing became shallow. The earth nurtured him through its gentle beating from below. It served only to accelerate the onset of a dangerous sleep in the hypothermic conditions. Angus was losing ground…or was he?

A stone fell down the granite rock face and thudded, muffled by the foliage. The Malakhim or guardian angel was back checking up on Angus as he drifted off to sleep. If Angus had been awake then he would have heard the guardian angel's wings buffeting together as it flew over him and down the mountain. The Malakhim was searching

94

out the four stags which had inspired Angus four years previous lower down on the mountain. It found them huddled together sheltering in the bleak night. The stags knew the angel naturally as it had been to see them on other occasions. They knew the angel like sheep know their shepherd. The Malakhim worked with God to help all creatures including humans. But what happened had already been foretold and this was something that the stags recognised in a way that was imperceptible to us. Soon they were up on their hooves, out of the bracken padding through the newly fallen snow and moving towards where Angus lay. Steam rose from them in the silence. The guardian angel disappeared leaving a golden silhouette. The four stags walked on for they knew their purpose.

Through the desperate cold of the night Angus retreated into the inner recess of his soul. Images impressed upon his psyche from bloody-faced demons to beautiful women. His world flashed before his mind's eye and his past trauma swirled like a bottle of whisky being flushed down the sink. The gossamer angel skin protected him from the biting cold but still the temperatures dropped unnaturally. His hair, which pushed outside of his angel skin hood, froze hard to his head contorting his face into an angular death grimace like a corpse in the bracken before it's time. Angus was in trouble. But then the stags arrived inconceivably herded to Angus by the Malakhim. They let him sleep on aware of his predicament. Angus had gone so far down inside himself he knew nothing of their approach. He just watched pictures like he was sat in the front theatre of his own mind. He was struggling to get back to reality. There was another time when this had happened outside Rosslyn Chapel when his saviour had been Vanessa Bermodes playing her part in the symphony of his hidden hand of fate. But that was assigned to the deepest caverns of Angus's mind. Calmly the stags lay down around him. Before Angus felt their warmth, he felt their souls. They settled and scented the iced air for the foul smell of the enemy, ever wary of them. They shuffled closer, pulling themselves in with their sturdy hooves. Angus felt comforted surrounded by their antlered presence even after the deep dive to his soul's heart.

The biggest stag stretched out its neck bringing its great head nearer to Angus breathing its steamy breath over his mouth. Quickly the pictures in his mind changed to those of mountains and bracken and the raging battering seas of over the lands of Clan Mackay near the House of Tongue. Angus could see the essence of the plants and medicating herbs which the big stag had been eating. Steam continued to rise from the stags as they attended Angus. The brown fur of thick deer hair scratched against his outer clothes. The four stags were charged with conveying to him his connection as a living entity to the planet. After the big stag finished it moved back in the bracken and the next stag moved its head close to Angus's face. A message conveyed from every growing hair on its fine head informed him of the deep connection of all living things and that the supreme intelligence was in everything. The second stag had been feasting on the psilocybin mushrooms abundant in these parts. Angus began to feel the Grail bowl and the scrapings from it which he'd put in his bath at Angela's in London. Somehow, through that, he'd accessed the secret to his next move returning to the world from where he'd been. It was a world that could well have been an illusion. Angus felt the situation in the essence of his soul as the breath of the stag caught in his nostrils and all the receptors in his brain started to work in unison. The way it worked was like this. When a person is being treated medically in the New Babylonian way it is called allopathic. This means that the components of the drugs he is prescribed, used to treat a certain condition, have been isolated specifically from the sum of their herbal parts to treat the condition. Whereas a person who is being treated homoeopathically benefits from the full value of all the components of the plant as it is all used. And there was a supernatural dimension to this that was not meant to be understood. That's exactly what was happening to Angus as his neurotransmitters were naturally reformatted by the micro-dose of magic mushrooms. The stags had tutored him by working together to heal his broken mind caused by the beast system of the New Babylonians which drives many to death. It was nothing new to know that the beast system, from which he'd escaped, caused his brain to malfunction as a consequence of the way he'd been 'in the box' educated which was furthered by the problems caused by his New Babylonian wife. Angus learned the hard way of how that process, he'd left in a world of long ago, was responsible for his mental outage. Somehow all of this had caused him to desperately seek a higher purpose and path. This was something, though, which was happening supernaturally as Angus cried out for help in the dark night of his soul on the mountain.

The third stag shuffled round like the other, almost crawling into place. It breathed on his face. The other two stags, having served their purpose, waited steaming in the cold around Angus in the frosted heather. The third stag breathed in a rhythm which sounded more like a musical instrument than anything else. Somehow the resonance created in the beast's body began to waken Angus from his mind tomb drawing him back into the now after healing his neurotransmitters now charged with God's energy from the Earth. He couldn't remember waking if indeed he'd even been asleep. But what he saw with the fourth stag confirmed God's plan.

The fourth stag shuffled round and began to rise up standing on its hooves enveloped in a silver light shining from a cross between its antlers. Then it opened its great mouth and bellowed and spoke.

"Angus you are fixed now to dwell in the present. But from here you will learn of the irregular nature of reality. Now go to the Loch below and look for the woman that swims under the sea." If this was death then Angus wanted more. But it wasn't, he was simply casting off the life patterns which had not served his purpose.

Having gone through an ascension-like process in the dawn, Angus woke from his ordeal in the remote car park at the bottom of Loch Eriboll. He was renewed again.

The frozen land started to melt as warmer air circulated like a draught along the ground. Angus raised himself into a sitting position brushing away the gravel which clung to his outer clothing. He recalled back to when he was in London under Tower Bridge when the River Thames lapped against his shoeless feet in the year of his penance. Loch Eriboll shined silver in the morning. He got up as if rising from a bed of treacle, for he had almost died again, but this feeling soon lifted.

In the distance he could see an old Land Rover chugging down the main track road which went round the Loch. There was a steady madness to the vehicle like it was aiming to drive off a cliff. The Land Rover's lights went out and it turned toward the car park entrance squealing to a halt crunching the surface gravel. A large woman got out in a Scandinavian hat with tassels. Angus already knew who she was and why she was here. He looked up expectantly as though he should have known her. She had initially not seen him camouflaged amongst the heather on the outskirts of the car park. She went round the back of the Land Rover and opened its clunky back door. She wrestled out some specialised diving equipment onto the ground. Angus walked a bit nearer behind her. She was totally absorbed with the tasks at hand. As she turned round Angus shuffled a bit closer. And then the women saw Angus. "Jesus you're here already?" She said dropping the diving gear.

"Och' sorry I should na' sneaked up on ya'."

The lady considered Angus carefully. She was not intimidated. She may have looked like a rufty tufty professional underwater specialist but there was more to her than that. She cracked a smile. "Ah yes you are here again, I dreamt about you last night." She knew that the situation was destined.

It was early on the Loch as seven geese spanked their wings against its glass like surface honking enthusiastically, their orange webbed feet paddling along the surface just before gaining height. "Ya' dreamt about me last night then" Angus said incredulously.

"Yes, but don't let it affect your ego; it was entirely different to what you are thinking?"

"Och' nay' bother, the idea never even entered ma' head." Angus remarked tightening his belt.

"Haha, Angus you fell for that didn't you? You thought I was some kind of Amazonian women predator?"

She was totally different to Angela Kirkbride, his friend from London. He even knew what this lady was going to say next.

"By the way my name is Angela Kirkbride. I am the part time conservation officer on the Loch. I also do a lot of diving particularly on the numerous wrecks laying down on the bottom."

"But if you've been here since 1988 that would make you too old to be here in ya' capacity as warden?"

Angela said nothing. It was like she'd missed the question. Like there was something bigger to contemplate than just another date enquiry.

She pointed downwards with her large tallow hand. It was a hand which looked strangely like the prophetic hand which turned over the pages of his bible in his den under the steps of Tower Bridge. A prophetic hand which pointed at random bible verses foretelling Angus of what was to come. Angus wanted to ask her something.

"There's the wreck of the German submarine down there, UB96 that's what I've come for today." Angela looked purposeful. "Let's just say it's what I came back for."

"Ya' mean ya' diving on a wreck today then?" Angus saw himself walk round to the side of this new type of Angela Kirkbride. When she moved away to the side, he saw her from above as if he was floating above her out of his body.

"There's lots of German submarines down there aren't there Lassie?"

"Last night you were in my dream Angus. And in that dream you were holding that supernatural sword. It was a sword so hard and sharp it could cut through diamond stalactites as if they were paper."

Angus looked at Angela and although she appeared nothing like his friend from London she had a similar essence. The size between the two ladies if indeed they were separate humans was disconcerting. Angus stepped back awkwardly. He'd suffered much on the cold mountain and was unable to think straight.

"Och' if you knew where I've been all night ya' would not be so eager to take on the icy coldness of Loch Eriboll out there."

"All part of the job for God," she replied.

Angela looked over at the Loch putting her finger in her mouth and raising her hand in the air. "There's a slight easterly breeze coming in but no cause for concern. We need to go into the Land Rover and discuss the plan Angus dear." Angela thought about what Angus had said about the mountain. "By the way, I heard you had a visit on Eriboll mountain from four stags?"

Angus swooned. "This is getting stranger and stranger. Let's just say I had a very strange time with those four stags."

Angela pointed at her long wheelbase Land Rover. "Come on get into the ol' jalopy, there's some coffee and food inside."

This was a blessing as the fangs of hunger were biting Angus. He walked over and opened the Land Rover door on its clunky 1980's spring, clunking it open. Inside it was somewhat more advanced than the Land Rover's 1980's robust workhorse exterior suggested. Inside there was a computer workstation with military grade computer technology. He could even stand up in it. The roof had been raised and there was a skylight window with a high-powered solar panel. Angela followed Angus and began to narrate a running commentary.

"I mean, I came up here with nothing apart from this old banger Land Rover, which I was sleeping in whilst I did the conversion job on her. I even washed in the Loch for nearly a year just like my father and mother." Angela walked over to where there was a coffee machine shelved above a fridge. "Come on Angus what will you have?"

Och' I'll just take an Americano with sugar and milk. And whatever there is to eat would be great."

"Yes, sure Angus you've been up the mountain in sub-Arctic conditions, you must be famished."

Angela set the machine steaming in motion whilst opening the mini fridge door to find a sandwich for Angus.

"Sit down there at the campaign table, I'll bring it over."

Angus stooped a little and sat down at the large board table. Maps and ships' architectural illustrations of German submarines were sellotaped to the plastic surface. Angela had been making calculations next to them. Angus looked about with a feeling of being back in a retro 1990's film. Something wasn't adding up. Strangely her handwriting reminded him of the mad writing of his father. The situation Angus experienced up on the mountainside was enabling him to remember passed incidents with clarity. He knew that previous incidents and events were weaving themselves into the reality of the now.

"As you can see I've become rather an expert on WW2 German U-Boats. Not entirely my subject choice, I hasten to add, I'd rather be out with my dogs."

"Aye Lassie yar' no' backward about coming forward are ye?"

"Ok Angus let's continue." She said ignoring his outburst.

Angus sat down with his Americano as Angela put a large ham sandwich in front of him which he then ate ravenously. Angela waited for him to stop.

"We haven't got a great amount of time. The German submarines which surrendered here in 1945 were led by that German Admiral,

Junkers. And we want his submarine. His U-Boat was actually the sister vessel of the submarine captured by their particular sworn enemy."

"Aye I can tell you who that enemy is, none other than the Pirate Brethren of the coast and their partners the Knights Templar."

Angela tilted her head sideways inquisitively. Angus looked solemnly at her.

"And guess what? What if I told you that I lived at the City of Light in Chiloe, Chile? They captured several of the Third Reich top brass. Of course, most of them died either during the attack on the submarine or later after they'd served their purpose spilling the information on the New Babylonians. Och' it was horrible." Angus looked around as if searching for a whisky, continuing, "but there's still a lower ranking officer left alive who had been the U-Boat 96 secretary, not a bad sort as far as the Nazi go. And he's in a wheelchair now, well what's left of him."

"Bloody hell Angus you have been on an adventure haven't you." Angela said knowing already where he'd been and what he'd done previously. She just knew. In fact, she knew everything in the blink of an eye.

Angus snarled, deep in past thought, fixated on Reiner. "Och' he was a certain Lieutenant Reiner Gorst and 'would be' novelist. Although we know he was writing about what was happening in reality. Call it non-fecking fiction! The submarine was being stormed by rabid pirates who, after butchering most of the crew, then took all the art treasures from on board the submarine."

"You've really been through the mill Angus dear, haven't you?"

Angus' brow creased in thought. "Aye Lassie it feels like a dream now but I have been having some vivid recollections." He put his hand on his chin in contemplation. "I sound like a right fanny don't I?" He laughed at himself. Angela got up from the table and before Angus could object, she embraced him smothering him so he couldn't move.

"Aww Angus you need a hug."

She hunkered nearer and grabbed him closing her arms around him and kissed the top of his head. Angus squirmed uncomfortably but there was nothing he could do. Angela got down to business.

"Drink your coffee I've got something to explain. And by the way I don't know if you know anything about ley lines but UB96 was scuppered on the ledge where a prominent ley line passes under it?" Angela looked over at Angus to see if what she'd said had registered.

"Aye it feels very supernatural around this Loch. There's more going on than meets the eye." Angus said.

"That ley line is called 'the Dragon's Spine', supposedly inactive until UB96 landed on it." Angela looked out over the mist towards the ledge.

Angus saw giant serpents wriggling in his mind's eye. Quickly he switched his focus to a medieval effigy carving of one of the knights in the Temple. Stone was in his blood. There was a postcard of the effigy pinned to Angela's notice board. It was Sir Richardson with his left leg bent under him like the hanged man in the tarot pack. Sir Richardson was the bodyguard to the famous Marshal family who expedited the writing of Magna Carta. He had been a penitent knight serving twenty-five years in the saddle and like many of them, still fit for battle into his 60's, at a time when the average lifespan for a person was forty. These supernatural sleepers in stone would one day awaken to defend the people as they had once done in the flesh.

Angus sipped at his Americano pulling him into reality. Angela clicked her remote control and a white digital screen dropped down in front of them both. She pressed it again and the screen flashed on. A series of black and white images from World War 2 appeared next to a moving film of the German U-Boat Commander, Admiral Junkers. Junkers was surrendering happily to the British Royal Navy as the German black flags of capitulation fluttered in the background. The scene looked congenial enough as British and German submariners moved around together on the decks of their U-Boats as if they were on the same side. But then Junkers had been deluded into thinking the Third Reich would resurrect to fight USSR.

Technical information of the German submarines streamed in appearing under each one of the pictures which expanded on the centre of the screen. Both subs appeared, set in another scene in a blue azure sea off the coast of South Chile next to a refuelling facility, supplying German military and scientific staff.

"You see my dear Angus, what the German's did was fiendishly clever." Angela was ready to tell Angus what he'd been waiting to hear with his recalibrated brain circuitry after his spiritual ascension up on the mountain with the four stags. She continued. "Now, the two UB96's were carrying some of the most important works of sacred art on the planet robbed by the Third Reich from Jerusalem and Italy. But all those treasures combined could not compare to the main treasure on the U-Boat of Admiral Junker's, UB96, sunk and resting over there on that hidden ledge." Angela pointed over to the Loch again through the Land Rover's misty window. The outside temperature was

105

beginning to increase. Angela was aware her under water mission was nearing.

"For feck's sake get ta' tha' point lady ya' driving me insane." Angus shook his head in childish exasperation. "I am back here for a reason; everything is linked to our purpose against the New Babylonians."

"True and I know you had a fabulous Viking Sword. But this next Sword, which is your destiny to wield, is much more. For it has scythed through the higher realms against the enemies of God."

"Aye I had a feeling you were going to say that. But am' ready for anything." Angus looked distant. "Ya' know we just take it with a pinch of salt all that's happening, it's like being in a spiritual washing machine. There's much more at stake than we know."

Angus was eager to know why Angela knew so much about him and the worlds he was moving between. And then it occurred that it was like talking to another version of Angela in London, she was bound to know some things, but not others, but this two in one person was uncanny.

"It wa' be nice to understand why you kna' so much. Do ya' know where I've just come from?"

"Look, there's not much time. U-Boat 96 was captured by the illustrious Pirate Brethren back in your other world of South Chile. She was the sister submarine to the one scuppered over there in the Loch." Angela drew her hand across her throat implicating death. "But the real treasure, the Sword of Methuselah, had been switched from UB96 captured by the Pirate Brethren and placed aboard the one over there which the British thought they'd sent to the bottom of Loch Eriboll never to be seen again." Angela pushed her hair back over her

106

ears and continued. "Both submarines were heading for Chile but only one made it. As we know its sister vessel which was captained by Admiral Junkers turned back. It was probably forced by divine providence to join the surrendering German U-Boats at Loch Eriboll. Admiral Junkers was deluded by the notion of joining the British to fight on against the Russians. He thought he would rise again with the British to continue the war against them."

"Och' aye, but if that's true why didn't Admiral Junkers remove the sword elsewhere?" Angus asked, digging further.

"That's a question I would have expected you to know the answer to Angus. And I've found no evidence of anybody knowing what was on board. The British navy searched the submarine like all the others, before it was scuppered. They brought out some interesting finds, but nothing like the Sword of Methuselah. I am sure the British Navy didn't have a clue about it." Angela hadn't finished her deductions... "I don't know why but I saw the Sword of Methuselah under the sea in a dream. I was told you needed it more than anybody else. Its hilt, by the way, has been carved into a weasel." There was a pause. "It's the only animal that can repel the horrible basilisk which all good people and animals fear."

"This is getting crazier and crazier" Angus replied shaking his head.

"The retro clock in the Land Rover's mobile office ticked noisily on the wall. Angus watched a cloud scud across the sky through the skylight. Momentarily Angus blinked. Angela became too faint to see like she was fading out of reality. "Are ya' alright Lassie?" He shook his head in frustration. "Where are ye' going?"

She spoke again reverting to full colour. "Divine providence Angus my dear, divine providence."

"You danna' sound convinced Lassie."

"I am as convinced as you were on the mountainside after your experience with those stags."

"How the hell did ya' know about them Lassie?" Angus had felt there was something ethereal about Angela from the start.

"I know as much about this situation as you do Angus. Each action, in reality, has a greater value somewhere else." Angus couldn't answer back. He knew she was on the same side, that's all that mattered.

"Y'er gonna' dive on the sub aren't you?"

"Yes of course I am. I already know the route in." Angela pointed out over the Loch. "The stern hatch where the crew came up to man their deck guns is still open. I've had a micro surveillance sub down there. Let's take a look here at the computer film." Angela flipped on the switch for the main screen and clicked the computer on. The screen lit up the footage of the German sub as if it were sleeping on the ridge before the murky depths. Large cod fish swam around it, flipping their tails and changing direction. A large conger eel pushed through the open hatch followed by an eruption of detritus and discoloration. With its bottom jaw pushed out like a bulldog it gaped menacingly in the oily sea. It was one of several others that had made UB96 its home.

Ma' God that's no for the faint-hearted Lassie." Angus said. "I wish I could come down there with you. But am no' specialist diver."

"You can man the station here and watch the film of my dive onto UB96. I shouldn't be long. Let's just say I've been preparing for this since I was born and perhaps even after I was dead."

"I wish there was more I could do." But then he started to think why she'd mentioned 'after she was dead.

"Oh come now Angus you've been preparing for your role and now I am preparing for mine."

She got up and began to prepare her diving gear. There was no dressing area. She pulled out her wet suit and began to take off her civilian clothes. Angus turned away. "Hey, there's no need for that false modesty Laddie." She blurted out kicking off her outdoor pants and top. Quickly she started to pull on the specialised wet suit, streamlining her profile. "Give me a hand this suit is like a straitjacket!" She kneeled before her oxygen tanks like kneeling before an altar. She turned on the air valves and tested the air input valve sucking in the air. "You can help me into the Loch. There's barely anybody around this time in the morning, it's too early and cold."

"Aye anything I can do ta' help." Angus picked up the specialised tank purposefully flattened to allow the diver access through narrow spaces. The downside of this tank was that it reduced her oxygen supply level by 30%. Angela had thought of everything including getting through the submarines stern escape hatch exit where they'd seen the large conger eel leaving. Putting the tank on his shoulder Angus opened the Land Rover door. Angela followed in her wet suit. She buckled on a saw-edged diver's knife. She had some diving fins specially adapted which she carried under her arm. There was barely

109

any flipper to them on account of her having to search inside narrow spaces where standard length flippers would encumber her.

"You're in charge of the Land Rover now. And don't worry the screen is already linked to my underwater cameras. All you have to do is help me into the Loch and keep an eye on the monitor."

"Och danna' worry I am a lot more high tech than you think."

Angela looked away unable to face Angus without laughing. "Take the landy keys and here's my bank cards and everything else you may need to carry on the fight if things go bad down there."

"Danna' be saying such things Lassie, you'll be coming back alright. Especially for that bottle of Johnnie Walker Whisky Black Label under ya' desk. Who would na' come back from tha' dead for that?! And even if yer' were dead it wa' soon bring ya' back to life." Angus said smirking.

She held out her arms as signal for Angus to lift the modified oxygen tank onto her back. He lifted it from the tarmacked car park where he'd positioned it ready on a trolley. Angela put her hands through the straps and then her arms and then forced her shoulders through the looped shoulder straps. She raised the oxygen tank's mouthpiece to her lips drawing in air and testing it again. Angus hooked his arm around her waist and she adjusted her helmet and fixed her goggle system. She raised her thumb in the air. He supported her in the modified weighted fins as she waddled forward into the Loch. Angus winced thinking of the cold she would face. Angela 2 checked her head camera and started the short swim to the Loch Eriboll ledge. She clipped a snap line onto her weighted bright orange belt. Her shoulders slipped beneath the green water surface and she turned round and gave

Angus the sign to start rolling the underwater camera. Angela had dived on the wreck of UB96 several times even once to dismantle the U-Boat's turret mast which was in danger of breaking the surface on uniquely low tides. Angela needed to stop unwanted attention.

She waved at Angus disappearing under the silver surface without a ripple. Angus clicked on his head monitor so he could see what Angela was seeing. The rusting bulk of UB96 was clear to be seen positioned precariously on a ridge in front of her. It was an anomaly why the sub had not been located by the plethora of amateur divers who frequented the Loch. This could be explained by the fact that UB96 was obscured by a large forest of Loch seaweed called bladderwrack camouflaging her from the direct vision of divers. Yet there was no other seaweed visible in the vicinity. Angus felt useless watching her go to fight his battle for him. But then, in essence, Angus needed the new sword...the Sword of Methuselah which they both knew was in UB96 according to his own intuition and Angela's prophetic dream.

She reached the forest of seaweed which swayed gently in the currents obscuring U-Boat 96. Now she swayed with this under water forest moving as if attached to the green fronds in the brackish waters. Bubbles rose to the surface about one hundred yards away across the Loch. She was nearly on her target. She plucked her head camera off her helmet and smiled into it showing her breathing apparatus. Angus laughed out loud and then with a heartfelt cry of admiration blurted out, "come on Lassie, you're the hero now, come on now!" Angela swam through the sea forest which surrounded UB96. It was only just possible to see her progress amongst the dark fingered fronds. Yet the turret tower of U-Boat 96 loomed above the forest of seaweed where Angela was slowly rising propelled by her modified fins. On the monitor Angus could see the seaweed forest moving like a rubber wall

111

in the gentle swell. It broke the surface only to surge back like a host of curious sea otters watching him. Angela pushed through it all slashing at it with her huge sea knife. She cut a path through to the UB96 turret tower, a reference point in the murkiness of the waters. Angus watched her change position to being almost diagonal to the deck of the UB96. She looked towards the submarine's stern. All was quiet down on the ledge save for the rising bubbles of her oxygen tank gurgling and bubbling upwards to the light. Angus adjusted the clarity on the console and as he did Angela turned to the stern searching for the open escape hatch. The disarmed deck gun had gone and all that remained was its support pinions. She part walked, part swam down the submarine clunking her weighted fins on the iron decks. She noted that the escape hatch cover lid was upright as it should be. She knew Angus would be watching so she flipped him a thumbs up. She didn't want to worry him. Angus flipped her 'a thumbs up' back at the screen on the console.

Something was worrying him though, like the feeling of entering a room where there might be a ghost. On either side of the submarine the forest of seaweed swayed backwards and forwards in the swell. Yet the Submarine's deck remained clear as a void in an everglade, apart from suede like algae more yellow than green, which carpeted the outer deck. She unclipped a high-powered underwater torch and glided along to the escape hatch. Warmer seawater came out of the escape hatch in tiny, discoloured swirls. Briefly Angela hung in the cloudy waters up above the entrance and began to descend into the submarine into the darkness until she switched on her thermal torch which illuminated the immediate space and substructure. In her dream she'd seen the cabin door of Admiral Junkers which was further inside towards the submarine's observation turret. Junkers, like most of the crew in their day, would be confined in small quarters on account of space efficiency required on an underwater war machine. However, if there was any more space to be allocated in the crew's quarters then it would be allocated to the Captain's cabin. Angela knew exactly where the eccentric Kriegsmarine Captain's cabin was. She'd been planning this for years even though, for part of that duration, she'd been dead.

After clipping her bright orange safety line to one of the escape hatch lugs, she pushed through, landing upright on the bulkheads. She looked down at the periscope fixed just before the tower turret. All the controls and consoles were covered in green sea algae with little eruptions of seaweed amongst it.

Further past the periscope where its extended handles were still in the outward position, Junkers cabin door remained slightly open. She couldn't be certain but she thought she saw it move. Half swimming half walking, she made her way down to the cabin door. There was a locker in Junker's cabin over his bunk, normally reserved for the captain's weapons in some of the plans she'd studied of the submarine's interior. The locker had been missed out from the drawings for some reason. This was where Angela had seen the Sword of Methuselah in her dream. She'd seen it fixed to the roof, so that if anybody had seen the hidden locker, then the sword had been disguised in such a way that no one could see it. She checked her oxygen levels and she had enough unless something unforeseen happened. But then she'd got a small emergency mini face tank clipped to her belt. It would give her enough time to get out and onto the surface of Eriboll. She scanned the torch along the submarine's murky control deck.

Something, though, had left swirling shapes imprinted in the algae, as if a large creature had been swimming along the steel floor, where its movements had been recorded in the detritus and algae. Bones of other sea creatures lay scattered about. The phenomenon passed over her. Angela pushed the cabin door open scanning the torch around the perimeter illuminating the single bunk and the nearby desk. She looked above the bunk and sure enough there was a locker above it. Still pinned to it was a black and white print Time magazine of the Temple of Solomon or what was left of it taken around 1940 in Jerusalem, suggesting that Junkers had some arcane interests of his own. Angela stood up, supported to some extent by the buoyant saltwater. She was aware that her time was running out in the submarine. She opened the locker further and shone the light inside. There was nothing in it apart from a pair of bloated leather sea gloves. But above the gloves was a leather case secretly fixed to the ceiling of the locker, just like she'd seen in her dream. It would have been almost impossible to see if it hadn't been for the high-powered diver's torch she shone on it. Indeed, if this was the Sword of Methuselah it wasn't very long. In fact, the famous Sword was of medium length curving dramatically with a carved animal hilt hard to make out in the clouded water. She reached into the locker for it. This sword felt heavier than it should have done for some reason. Then it was like someone pressed the emergency button. Back down the length of the submarine out through the escape hatch something was stirring with a growing rage of being deprived of its evil supernatural purpose. A giant conger eel nearly as thick as a telegraph pole and eight feet long was returning to what it guarded. This giant eel was larger again than the one that both Angela and Angus had seen earlier. Enraged, it thrust its bull like head down the U-Boat's escape hatch with a juddering echo which reverberated in the hollow drum of the dead submarine. Angela placed her hand on the large knife in readiness. She did not know what was coming until the cabin door burst from its steel hinges and floating inwards on the force with an eruption of particles muddying everything like an underwater sandstorm.

Saint Bridget and the Hands of God

A white feminine apparition appeared, expanding with flowing blonde hair as if blowing in the wind, in some other dimension under the Loch in Junker's cabin. Angela was calm as the illuminated figure fully manifested as a Saint. The Saint was trying to warn Angela with pleading hands. It was Saint Bridget or the Lady of the Lambs. Time stood still as the figure genuflected, holding out her arms pleading like a scene from a Baroque painting. No one knows what happens at the point of their death or who or what is sent to stave it off. Or what a person actually feels. Death is intimately different to each of us, depending on the way we have lived our lives. For it was a scenario she'd faced several times and been subject to it but once. It was enough to snap her into action. Angela drew her sea knife as the bull-like head of the giant conger eel thrust through the door with gaping jaws and jags of needle pointed teeth. Ominously it rose up to her on the bunk bed of Junkers where Angela transfixed, waited, holding her large knife defensively in front of her. She panicked and began panting out the last of her oxygen into her face mask. This was a situation which she'd not accounted for in her wildest dreams. With snapping alligator jaws the giant eel pushed closer and closer in the cloudy water. Inside its fowl mouth were several tongues, like those of snakes, slithering independently behind its jags of teeth. Angela reached for the Sword in the locker's ceiling again. As she did, the serpent eel grabbed her snatching at her leg and locking on. The pain was indescribable and encouraged by her spurting blood, it twisted its weight against her trying to finish her off. Angela, dredging up some fearful strength, plunged her knife into the skull of the monster. There was a slicing flesh noise. And then the knife stuck out of the serpent's skull like an antenna of steel, yet still it would not stop. Blue, red blood leaked out from it in streaks in the murkiness. Despairingly Angela kept focussed and checked her oxygen level. It was nearly spent but the serpent eel continued to move.

In the chaos, she was beautifully overwhelmed by a great sense of peace. And one could be forgiven for thinking that Angela was very much closer to Saint Bridget than ever. And now, it was not just Angus MacWilliam who would have the privilege of seeing the Hand of God. In the murky gloom Saint Bridget faded into the corner of the cabin, shrinking in size and bathed in a phosphorescent light. Fingers sprouted and quickly began to form into a hand. The fingers closed tight together, bending at the knuckles, so that its profile became like an animal head. Another two alabaster white hands formed, joining behind like shoulders. Then many hands developed with fingers like little legs and another sixty more, further behind. A larger hand formed in the cloudy sea. It turned and attached to the rear of the multi fingered monster like a giant centipede of flesh-welded-hands with a deadly stinging finger of sulphurous orange. The multi fingered form scuttled towards the serpent eel, rapidly engaging and squeezing it, tearing and squashing out its vitriolic life force. The serpent eel released Angela's leg enabling her to grab the Sword in its leather case from the inside of Junker's secret locker. Angela's blood still swirled cloudy red through the tear holes in her wet suit. Just as she grasped the Sword, the multi fingered form arched its back scorpion-like, and with supernatural velocity stung the serpent eel, severing the monster into two separate portions. Still twitching, its bulbous head thudded to the deck of the cabin, blood pumping out, still trying to tear Angela with its knitting needle teeth. Quickly the huge centipede of hands shrunk back to the size of a handkerchief, returning to the form of Saint Bridget, still pleading her prayer in the corner. Angela pushed

117

out of Junker's cabin, swimming down the operations deck towards the escape hatch. Her air supply was nearly finished. Fumbling she inserted the emergency mouth tank clipped to her belt. She then unclipped her oxygen tank belt and let it sink to the floor with one hand whilst still holding the Sword of Methuselah with the other.

She had no idea how precariously the submarine was perched on the ledge. The submarine groaned and juddered as it began to finally slip over the ledge into the abyss. Still bleeding she surged back up through the escape hatch. She pushed up and out of the submarine as it crunched and began to slip off the ledge. She followed her exhaled bubbles of oxygen up towards the shimmering light. She swam up pulling steadily away from the downward suction as UB96 headed for the abyss beneath. She looked down beneath her in the deep waters to see dull light emanating from the plunging sub. She thought she had seen a pair of angel's wings as well. And with fortitude she swam up for the light pulling for all she was worth. Angus could see the surface bubbling further out from where he stood helplessly. But Angela had won the Sword of Methuselah.

Meanwhile Angus had watched some of the battle on the computer console and was now being sick into the shallows on edge of Loch Eriboll. He'd had a flashback to the time in his safe haven under London Bridge during his 'penance of poverty' in the City. He'd never felt so useless. But he knew that once he'd got the Sword of Methuselah things would be different. He looked at the console screen to see Angela's eyes closed in concentration, pushing through the darkness towards the light. She spat out the spent mouth tank. She reached across for the Sword of Methuselah strapped to her back. Grabbing it with her right hand she held its handle and kicked for the surface. As she emerged, she thrust the sword triumphantly through the surface like the Lady of the Lake. From the shore Angus could see an arm raised high in the water holding the most powerful sword in the history of Man.

"Ma God she's got it! Oh ma' she's like the Lady of the Lake!" Angus blurted out in the stillness.

A persistent heron which lingered in the shallows launched in slow motion from the shore. Angela turned over and back paddled towards Angus. Around her a film of red blood discoloured the surface. Angus dropped the console screen on the shore and waded out to meet Angela. He grabbed her trying to get a grip of her slippery wet suit. "Och Lassie you're bleeding badly" Angus took off her scuba mask gently checking for signs of trauma. As he dragged Angela to the shore he saw her ripped wet suit shredded down one leg. There were three open puncture wounds on her leg.

"Come on Lassie I'll get you back to the Land Rover and we can fix you with the magic thread."

"Let me get some air Angus!" she replied urgently.

The thread Angus was referring to was an anti-bacterial potion impregnated into silver thread he'd brought from the other realm. Once he'd seen another knight stitched from his neck to his abdomen with the thread which healed five days later. They pushed his guts back in and stitched him up with two hundred stitches. Soon the knight was back in the saddle. Angus reached out for the sword of Methuselah. At first Angela was reluctant to pass it over.

"Ya' can keep it Lassie, am only trying to help ya'." Angela snapped out of it as she slipped on the rocks near the shallows. "Come on Lassie let it go."

"Take it Angus, it's yours now, take the Sword."

She passed it over her shoulder in the hard leather case. Angus took it thinking how light it was. He could see her claret-like blood clouding the seawater of the Loch behind. He helped her up into the Land Rover and pushed her onto the plastic operations table in there. Angus put the sword on one of the seats. Taking some scissors, he began to cut her out of her wetsuit to save her losing any more blood. It was clotting leaving globules on the rubberised Land Rover floor. Soon Angela was laying there in her sports bra and pants. Angus ignored the obvious and began to wash her down with warm water from the supply inside.

"These cuts are no' so bad, more like puncture wounds."

"Yes, its teeth were like needles." Angela replied.

Even so the punctures were bruising badly as he washed the blood away. Angus made her a cup of sweet tea from the same supply of hot water and gave it her. He sorted out the immediate problems and then started to stitch the wounds with his big-thumbed hands grabbing her thighs roughly.

"Not so rough Angus, this is agony," she said wincing.

"Aye, sorry Lassie."

Angus backed off admiring his handy work on the puncture wounds on her thigh. Already the punctures were glazing over and healing together. And then they both heard a noise coming from the sword. It sounded like a little bell ringing. Oddly, Angela seemed to take on the persona of 'posh Angela' from London who was slimmer, finer boned and not so brash. It was like looking at two versions in one flesh shell.

Angela 2 was obviously more tough and voluptuous than the slicker, smarter businesswoman of Angela 1 from London making her deals and organising money.

A jolt of extraordinary energy shook his mind.

"Och na! no' again, I feel dizzy, och' no' again!" He sat down gasping for air. Angela sat up on the operations table. Supernaturally her wounds had all but healed. Now there were only bruises.

"Look, take a drop of this!" Quick as a thunder flash she brought out the bottle of Johnnie Walker Black Label whisky. "Wash your tonsils in some of this."

Angus uncorked it and poured a flow into his coffee downing it in one. "That'll do Lassie I am back in tha' now."

"Look we have the sword, I know you are frightened of it Angus, who wouldn't be. But I think you should at least take a look at it." Angela looked at her leg as the dreadful wounds healed. "You'll be needing the sword soon enough." As she spoke the weather darkened and a huge air pocket bubbled up on the surface of the Loch as wreckage from UB96 broached the surface in an oily slick.

"What the hell was that!" Angus asked. Angela sat forward looking out over the Loch from the Land Rover's little window.

"My God it looks like UB96 has come back to haunt us. Look its spewing its innards out. That will have the local eco people out as fast as rats out of a fire. You gonna' have to drive us out of the way. We can keep our heads down over at my place for a while."

Quickly Angus stepped over to where the Sword of Methuselah was on the seat. He looked down and began to reach for it. As he did a magnetic force from the sword made it fly into his open hand. Angus' eyes widened. Then he took it from the Egyptian ram skin scabbard. Angus could see the curved blade. He received flashbacks from its past as he took ownership of its energy. The sword lopped off the heads of those who had stood against God and its shiny cobalt edge slashed open the veins of the damned. The Methuselah sword worked from a deeper realm, a place where the Spirit of all Living Things dwelt fortified with a higher power. And that power was Light: Light of the World, the Light of Heaven, the Light from God's Eyes. He had created an incredible cutting edge, designed to slash both the evil inside and the flesh outside. For the Methuselah Sword was as much a sword of the spirit as it was a cutter of flesh. Angus pulled it out of the golden threaded scabbard and gasped, for the blue ambient sword revealed a perfectly carved weasel hilt.. Angus trembled with gratitude. carefully sliding it back into the scabbard. Angus walked over and examined Angela's wounds which were now nothing but faint bruises.

"Where's the keys hero lady? I'll get us moving to where we need to go."

"The keys are in the ignition; switch on the sat nav we need to get round the other side of the mountain where I have a little hidey hole of a croft."

Angus jumped into action and slid through to the driver's seat turning over the big Perkins' diesel engine, bringing it into thundering life. Angela got up and pushed through into the passenger seat.

"Hey lady, be careful you've only just been mauled by a horrible giant eel," Angus said turning over the Land Rover in preparation to set off.

"Ok good, come on man let's go," Angela replied.

They set off driving onto the main Tongue Road, which led to the turn off where the track was for Angela's croft. After about ten minutes of peaceful motoring a dark lane appeared with excessive growth of bracken, untamed after years of neglect. From 1850, after the Highland Clearances, humans were purposely replaced by sheep and said to be 'more cost effective' by their landlords. It was indeed one of the most disgraceful periods in British history. Angela's croft had been included in this ghastly regime only to be repurposed and rebuilt by Angela's stoic father, Dougal Kirkbride, years later.

Now Angus could see the mountain path above, leading to the ancient Wheelhouse structure, high on top of the obscured plateau, as they bounced down the track in the unyielding Land Rover.

"I hope this jolting about no' hurting them wounds ma' lady." he said rumbling down it. Angus noticed the bright orange and blue lights of the rescue services swooping in on the Loch from both the air and from the loch itself. The situation hadn't got past Angela either.

"Don't worry Angus, it will take them a while to find out what has been happening under their noses."

"Aye, well now Lassie, they will nay' catch up with us."

They continued lurching from side to side down the track on the old potholed road towards Angela's homestead. Or at least that's what Angus was expecting. He was looking forward to a proper bed for the night and a decent meal.

Another mile into the damp Highland landscape there was nothing apart from dense overgrown hedgerows, set against borders of random rocks that had been cleared from the land for planting oats and potatoes. Later those who had cleared the rocks were also 'cleared out' by their so-called landlords to make way for sheep. New generations here were generally incomers or returning romantics like Angela. There was a walled garden further down the track and there were signs of much older buildings nearby. At least that was what Angus was thinking. And he'd not yet seen the leaning gravestones amongst the bracken and died down ferns.

They pulled up outside the main croft which hadn't changed in two hundred years. Some years back she'd put a roof on the croft house and done some rebuilding, doing most of the work herself. The windows were original sash windows pilfered from the local redundant lighthouse keeper's cottage down on Eriboll years ago. Although Angela's family had originally been local crofters, she'd escaped that harsh life by running away to London as soon as she'd finished agricultural college, only to return to take on the croft a few years later. Angus looked at the croft feeling uneasy by the sense of melancholy coming from it. Angela leant forward as if she was listening to something. She had the peaceful countenance of someone at a classical concert.

"I won't be a minute Angus, I'm just going in to let the dogs out before they make a mess." Angela started to unbuckle her seat belt, opening the clunky sprung-loaded handle grimacing.

"Be careful Angela ya' wounds are not quite healed. Danna' let them dogs jump all over ya'."

Whether it was his imagination or some development of it, Angus thought he saw a look of 'otherworldliness' wash over Angela's face. Like the look of a person in hospital with a terminal illness, resigned to the fact death was approaching. He'd seen that look in several friends and relatives over the years.

He heard wings flapping together lightly, ever so lightly. Now the wind had dropped and there was a feeling of being in a spiritual place like outside a Temple or Church.

He sat there a while and decided to go inside to see if he could help her. He wondered why Angela hadn't called him inside. He listened out for the barking of the dogs anxiously. He hung the sword of Methuselah on its belt over his shoulder for safe keeping. He got out of the Land Rover and walked over to the old croft door which he'd seen Angela go through. There was no barking. And to make matters worse the croft door was padlocked from the outside. Astounded he jumped back. "Fa feck' sake, what's goin' on."

He tried to force the front door but it was a solid built cottage door and not for budging. In a moment of panic Angus picked up a bent iron bar he'd seen on the ground. It was a makeshift crowbar which he immediately levered against the padlock hasp. He put his whole body behind it and soon the lock hasp burst from the door with a cracking bang of splintering wood around it. He pushed the door open which scraped along the Caithness flagstones as if it had not been opened for years.

"Angela. Angela, where are you, if this is some kind of joke?" Nothing came back, not even the barking dogs. The croft appeared not to have been lived in for years. Angela had made a point of explaining about her home. But it was an explanation from thirty years previous which matched the few household objects from that time lying about. There was a pair of old platform shoes and a copy of the 90's magazine Vendo and old vinyl records of Duran Duran. There was bright zany coloured, patterned wallpaper peeling from the walls. The items from the past were clothed in spider webs which also clouded the windows inside. And the flagstone floor was covered in almond shaped rat droppings. There was a dead bird lying on the worn-out chair near the fireplace and the back door was wide open. In fact, it had been open since 1998. Mummified dead birds looked like stick puppets poking out of the soot in the fireplace. In a corner of the tumbled down room there was a metal bowl used to feed dogs and there was a pair of dog leads hanging up behind the front door he'd just forced open. Water from the leaking roof had dripped down the leads leaving discoloured streaks over the rest of the door. But where had Angela gone?

He went over to a table where, thirty years ago, a family had sat down to a cup of tea and a piece of shortbread, or taken porridge with a wee dram in it for breakfast. On the table there was a paper. It was testimony to a person for a church service. He could see the cross and some roses illustrated on it. He picked it up and began to read it aloud.

"Angela Kirkbride, died aged 25. She was the deeply beloved daughter of Mr and Mrs Kirkbride of Croft Fold, Loch Eriboll A good soul of Christ and time-honoured ranger of the Eriboll National Park. Miss Kirkbride died doing what she loved most, diving on the wrecks of German submarines."

Angus ceased reading right away. He was having difficulty breathing. There was a picture of Angela Kirkbride as a slim girl stood in a wet suit holding World War 2 German military weapons. She had retrieved these from the various submarines she'd explored as a diver. He lurched for the front doorknob grabbing it and jerking it back, scraping the door along the stone flags. It was humid and misty in the croft and he needed air after what he'd seen. The situation was further compounded by the fact that Angela's Land Rover had gone, or at least moved. It was now over in the bracken, or perhaps the bracken had grown around it in some supernatural way. In any case what Angus saw was now a ruined, discoloured Land Rover. It had broken springs and windows and smashed mirrors. How could this be? Angus walked over to it. After peering through the windows he realised it was the same one, exactly the same version, now ruined by the environment and legions of nesting animals which could only have happened over decades.

Now there was something that drew Angus to the dry stoned wall garden further along. In fact, he felt guided to it. He looked up skyward as it began to spot droplets of salt laden rain. He walked to the beaten down track, kicking out at the thorns which infested the ground, passing Angela's old cottage and an outbuilding. He went over to the little walled garden which was calling him. He entered the tumbled down boundary wall and walked through the makeshift kissing gate to see several tombstones. He realised it was like a home-built graveyard with large tombstones leaning over dramatically as from a Dickensian style horror story. The activity of worms over the years had tilted the gravestones and there was nobody left to tend them.

In the rain and failing light the tombstones gathered a kind of mordant energy. Angus had been getting quite fond of Angela. But something wasn't right. He walked a step closer to the group of headstones. He bent down and rubbed the main tombstone which was covered in algae and discoloured. The stone had some lovely plain lettering which, as an ex-stonemason, he admired. He pushed his fingers delicately into the v-cut incision of the words not knowing what it said until, that is, he recognised the name of Angela Kirkbride. It seemed the funeral testimony on the table in the croft was correct in some way despite his denial. For complete confirmation he read out the inscription on the tombstone.

Angela Kirkbride

Born March 1970 - Died March 1995

Taken young on Loch Eriboll doing what she did best. Deep sea diving on the wrecks of Britain's past enemies. Sadly missed by all

Once more unto the mighty sea

Angus turned ashen, feeling like a washed-out rag. He then noticed the last line of the inscription. It was a quote by the great writer Horace which said, 'Once more unto the mighty sea.'

In fact, that quote had also been used by Angus's own father who died in Canada about the same time as Angela Kirkbride or seemingly the second version of her according to the date on her headstone. Angus broke down collapsing onto the green kerbstones close by her grave.

"Och' naw', this is happening again and again; wha' sort of a game is this God?!"

Blubbering and spewing Angus knelt over the grave of Angela Kirkbride. To make matters worse the two smaller head stones either side of hers had been carved with the names of her dogs, *'Brisco and Beth died of broken hearts aged 9 and 10 for want of their mistress'*.

Yet in the gloom God had sent him a consolation prize. Angus, as a mere human, could not comprehend the depth of God's wisdom in this situation. Nor could he comprehend God's reach through time to equip him with the sacred sword. He looked back round to the little lover's gate where he now saw a pair of twinkling eyes looking over from the ground.

Angus looked one last time at Angela Kirkbride's tombstone and then remembered back to when he was a boy, across on the Pentland Firth fishing and rowing. As a youngster he'd gathered seaweed when walking along the rugged coast of Caithness opposite the Isle of Stroma. He had a dog then, a wee terrier which followed him everywhere called Fazzer. The fierce terrier even went fishing with him. A familiar pair of eyes glinted in the half-light by the kissing gate. It had been thirty-five years since his braw ginger terrier had been by his side. He remembered when Fazzer jumped out of the skiff to chase a seal in the strong current. The mad terrier disappeared under the swell only to reappear twenty yards away from the boat. Angus rowed out to him and managed to grab him by the scruff of the neck. He knew the connection humanity had with animals is all part of the living God.

Sword strapped over his shoulder, he considered his next move as he walked away from Angela's tombstone, reluctantly accepting what had happened. She was the lady who'd retrieved the most important weapon, The Sword of Methuselah, to fight the demons. And then he discovered she'd been dead for thirty years. Not easy, not at all easy! Angus put his hands together in prayer. It was the only thing to do.

As the moon rose over Loch Eriboll, Angus thought about climbing the mountain back to the Wheelhouse portal where the demon army would emerge. It was known that the demons would terrorise everyone starting in the far north in Scotland raping, pillaging and stealing souls along the way. And after causing untold fear in all the people, they would focus on going after those persons who had defied the mandates; especially those unmarked and non-compliant. Angus's task was to delay the demon army with the Sword of Methuselah as the Army of God came through the Portal in the Temple in London.

He walked back out of the little graveyard and there was Fazzer sat wagging his stumpy tail, back from the dead. How could this be? A long time ago he'd buried Fazzer on the side of Eriboll which had been a day of tears. Now the dead were helping Angus. All was like a fractured glass kaleidoscope of past scenes from his life which returned to form a picture of reality. Previously he'd seen time as linear, organised by the now, the past and the future. Currently he was seeing time as a fractal pattern of multi-dimensionality, connected somehow to one higher power. It was all part of the battle for reality and escaping from the models established by the New Babylonians. These models placed humanity in a time scale meant to enforce their productivity for those who controlled them. Endeavouring to be optimistic Angus leaned forward offering the terrier his outstretched hand.

"Come Laddie, it canna' be you, ya' wee scruff," and he patted Fazzer's head lovingly as he'd done as a boy.

He realised there was no point staying at the broken-down croft any longer. He didn't question the reality of his situation anymore. He just went with the flow. And he set off with Fazzer at his heels climbing up the rear mountain path leading to the Wheelhouse moon observatory. At last, he drew the fabled sword carefully from its scabbard. Anyone without permission to use it would have been obliterated by now. The medium length of the sword was not his normal choice of blade. On further examination he realised it was

130

made of extremely hard composite material more like stone than metal. He flicked the sword with his fingernail and it rang like a bell. A strange inscription just appeared on the cross-guard which he recognised as ancient Hebrew. 1717 came to mind because the letters resembled the shape of those numbers. Angus realised that this form of lettering represented the name of God or Yahweh יהוה, also known as the Tetragrammaton. The sword began to resonate as he lifted it. It was made of transparent stone.

Angela 1 from London Arrives Back

Then Angela Kirkbride, version 1, from the posh end of London appeared. He was really grateful to see her standing there on the upward path. The last time he'd walked this mountain with her was fifteen years ago and they'd taken the official route which was opposite to the one they were on. Now she stood there with her dark hair in a red top and shoulder bag and not at all dressed for walking over difficult ground. Instead, she looked like she was ready for a posh shopping trip.

"I thought you were staying in London hen ya' not dressed for the mountain. I should have known you'd show up back here at some point."

"Angus, I told you before when we were on the Embankment in London not to call me hen!" She smiled which Angus took as affirmation that she was comfortable in the sub-arctic settings. It was as though she was in two places at once.

"Och sorry I forgot."

He'd taken the trouble to pack a small hip flask full of Johnnie Walker Black Label whisky he had found in the other Angela's converted Land Rover. He wasn't convinced that both versions of Angela were just the same person. He just couldn't tell. Angus could smell the deep whisky aroma from the hip flask. His lips were numbed pleasantly by the golden nectar as it slipped into his mouth.

"Ahhh' lovely," he uttered in the calm of the cold evening.

"Still liking the whisky Angus eh?" Angela asked smiling. Come on give me a swig!"

"Aye a' still fancy a drop now and again. We need the water of life from time to time." He stretched out his hand holding the flask out to her. Angus now accepted this new type of time along with all that was happening around him.

"Look my man, even though I am bloody freezing, I think I've been sent to help you somehow."

"Aye danna' tell me Lassie."

Angela looked down on the little ruined croft where Angus had come from.

"Angus I've been told you are not ready just yet for further development. You'll never believe this, but I had Andrew Sinclair come over for a drink of wine in London. Yes, you know the one and we had rather too much Châteauneuf du Pape." Angela grew solemn. "The thing is, I think it was his ghost."

"Och Lassie, I can never get hold of him when I need him you must remember us going to his apartment overlooking the Thames?" But in the archives of his mind, he realised that the word ghost really meant alive somewhere else.

"Listen carefully, Andrew told me two things. He told me you have the Sword of Methuselah and that another lady with exactly the same name as me got it for you. Call her my 'other self' just to simplify things."

"Aye it's a struggle getting ma' scone round that."

"She'd a terrible battle under water with a giant serpent, and I saw an elemental force from God manifested to kill it, comprising of hundreds of hands." Angela 1 confirmed.

"Aye a ken' what you're talking about. I watched a bit of the fight in Junker's cabin from Angela's underwater head camera."

"I know Angus, but it was like I was there as well somehow. Like I too was part of Angela; like I was there with her and that horrid serpent thingy. It's the last time I ever eat fish!"

"Och' yes love, true but ya' know I never liked that fish soup in London we used to eat."

"Nothing like telling it as it is eh Angus?" said Angela 1 laughing.

"I'm only here for a while. I've got some shopping to get at Harrods," she said looking fay in the incongruous setting of the bleak Eriboll mountain. "So, let's get down to business. Andrew told me about the great demon army." She sighed hesitantly. "Wooa' I sound like I am in some kind of video game promotion," and then she fanned herself with trendy emotional flapping hands.

"Come on Lassie what's the crack?"

"The great demon army is coming soon. You must stop them coming through the portal at the Wheelhouse with the Sword of Methuselah. This will buy time for the Templar and Pirate Army."

"Aye that will be right, I'm ready Lassie."

Angela could see the famous Sword hanging sheathed over Angus's shoulder. "And that is why you've got the sword," she said focussing on it. "You've got to get up there, because by first light they'll be

134

stomping through the stone arches hell-bent on destroying everything on their way down to London. Unfortunately, the Army of God was delayed getting through to their portal station from that other place. You left them early and the demon army unleashed horrendous creatures of destruction upon them. We had to make a strategic retreat." Angela 1 stared into the dull bracken between her boots.

"Aye I know Lass, the Army of God is coming through the Temple portal in preparation to defend London and take down the New Babylonians at the same time. It's our only chance. The New Babylonians are controlling the demon army not the other way around." Angus hadn't finished. "And the central hub of control is now what we once knew as Parliament. And look how they've been twisted by the bad spirit of Babylon." There was now something of the prophet about Angus. "You see it's the downward spiralling spirit of humanity that allows the demons to come into the world and in a way, we are all responsible for that."

Angela looked out of place on the cold mountain side.

"The most important thing you can do now is just get back up the mountain and do your job. As you know I am just the messenger." Angela looked down at his ginger terrier Fazzer. "Follow your old dog it knows the second path back up the mountain. That's why he's come back. It wasn't easy putting him back together again. Animals are mostly not keen to return to this life. However, love for his master oiled the machinery of the universe shall we say? It's all part of the plan."

Angus pushed his coat sleeve over his moistening eyes.

"Och' danna' make a big deal about it. But 'am ready let's get on wi' it." He tightened his jaw and moved forward.

Angela came over pushing herself into his chest. It was a perfect fit. In fact, guiltily he thought back to the same fit he'd had with Vanessa Bermodes his one-time wife. Angus bent his neck downward pushing his lips towards her and thinking back to the ecstasy a kiss could give, which he wanted more than ever. Every man from time to time wants to lose himself in the flesh of the lips. And then ping! she just vanished leaving Angus clawing at the air like he was on the edge of the mountain. It was like she'd never been there.

Angus cried out into the stillness. "Where are ya' fa' feck sake?" Fazzer pattered up along the path stopping only to look back as if waiting for Angus. It was time for him to do his job. Angela 1 had returned to London.

The ascent up the other path above Eriboll, although steeper, was a faster route to the Wheelhouse portal on the top. Angus needed to be up there by six o'clock the following morning. He strode out along the pathway and as he did he began to draw the Sword of Methuselah knowing it would act as illumination. He grasped the bone handle, feeling the sacred carvings adorning it from biblical times. The carved weasel on the hilt was there to protect the wielder of the sacred blade. The sword was smaller than Angus's famous Viking Ulfberht blade being kept by the knights and pirates. It was said that only those destined to wield this biblical sword in earnest would be able to draw it. As he drew it, Angus admired the perfectly curved symmetry of the blade. The blade worked by bringing about huge, centralised increases of kinetic energy against the enemies of God through the power of resonance. On the appearance of its enemies the sword would burst into flames and the sacred carvings on the handle would protect the wielder from them. Angus needed the light from it to help get to the top of the mountain by early morning. He held it out in front of him until it started to resonate a little. The blade lit up the space around him with phosphorus ambience. Fazzer was scampering up the path in the distance, as he'd always done when Angus was a boy.

As he walked, he drifted back to better days when the world seemed normal; tough but normal. It was a time when people had respect for life and what it brought them. He remembered fishing for his supper and digging up tatties to boil and sitting down at the table with his old mother before she became seriously ill. Enjoyment back then had been sitting in front of an open fire reading his favourite book. And then he'd had to go to Canada to better himself. Like a switch going on, everything changed as the totalitarianism of mass surveillance and control of the people's information began. This was when the malignancy began but, in actual fact, the situation had been planned for many years. Now Angus was looking at fighting it with a biblical sword and a dog back from the dead. He looked back over the little ruined crofting stead he'd come from, where the vastness of Loch Eriboll shimmered behind, illuminated by the moon. The path glowed with the low light coming from the Sword strangely pairing itself to fit Angus's large hand. He thought of the past and how straight and simple everything had been. Most of those he'd grown up with had been poor but of good health. Now there was much decadence and moral degradation which seemed to operate hand in hand with the 'beast system', as he'd come to call it. More people were sicker than ever. And not only that, people were being harmed by huge doses of electro-magnetic frequency radiation; a weaponised communication system designed to cause all manner of illness and death.

Angus continued climbing steadily and as he did he watched the moon drift across the night sky. Fazzer guided the way and after three hours of gentle walking they stopped by a spring and drank from it. The gurgling of the water was peaceful in the lightly illuminated evening. His journey down from the mountain after his arrival through the Wheelhouse portal had been mentally cleansing, removing the pollution of his life under the New Babylonians. What he'd thought was a neurological problem was in fact the poison inflicted on him from his existence amongst the New Babylonians. Fazzer scurried ahead showing the path to Angus as he neared the top of the mountain. Angus had been walking for hours and not known it. The demons that Angus would have to face at the Wheelhouse required him to have newly designed armour. Special times required special tools.

Dressed Like a Pangolin

First, Angus's woollen fisherman's hat disappeared, changing to a mailed coif hood of vitrified jade segments, stretching onto his shoulders,. Next his fleece top disappeared and was replaced by a woven metal copper wire tabard of segmented jade armour. The armour was designed to protect him from demon venom. He kept wearing the Malakhim undergarment as part of the new armour system. The jade armour went down his legs enabling him to move like a pangolin. Now he looked like a giant pangolin. All that remained was for the helmet he was destined to wear, to appear. As he approached the upper level of the path, Angus saw the Wheelhouse structure from the rear side ascent above him. As soon as Fazzer saw the top, he'd done his job and he simply disappeared back to his grave over the brow. Strangely Angus felt no pain; he had learned to accept his new 'flow state' amongst the kaleidoscope pictures of time from the other places of his reality. Fazzer had just returned to a state of peace having done his job.

Angus began to prepare. He fixed his leather sword belt to allow the Methuselah Sword to hang down on his right side ready to be drawn by his left hand. The Wheelhouse stood out against the light of the half-moon. A gap appeared in the ether. A large shell structure appeared in front of him. Angus remembered seeing such a form in the sketch books of Leonardo da Vinci. It glinted with silver and blue ethereal streaks punctuated all around with small holes. The abalone shell drifted closer to him. To all intents this was a very strong sophisticated helmet formed naturally in the sea. The abalone shell is reputed to be the strongest of all nature's composite structures. God was offering Angus a new war helm made to go with his lightweight pangolin scaled armour. It seemed that if Angus was going to stand alone against the great demon army, then God would make sure he had the best armour ever devised. Over the helmet itself was a thin skin of the protective anti-demon bile gossamer. The helmet slowly lowered onto Angus's head as if he'd been measured for it as it fit perfectly. The protective silk stuck to his face like wet cloth, arranging itself and becoming integrated with his flesh.

Angus drew the Sword of Methuselah and walked towards the Wheelhouse portal surrounded by the ancient henge stones. The segmented jade sections made no noise as he went. The holes in the abalone helmet gave him one hundred and eighty degree vision. And even though his face was covered by the gossamer material it was like he never had it on. The gossamer material transmuted into his flesh directly.

"Aye 'am ready now, come on now, show ya'self, ya' pile of pukey demons." His words rang out in the silence like a bell in a desert.

Now Angus needed to be the Grail Knight fuelled with righteous anger. He prepared himself to repel whatever came up out of the pit. As Angus drew the sword a copper wire fell from its scabbard. Then the segments of his pangolin armour began to vibrate unpleasantly with the rumbling coming up through the Wheelhouse portal. He realised what he must do, remembering. Bending down he pushed the screw-like head of the copper-coloured strip into the ground and then wrapped the other end round the Sword of Methuselah. The trembling under the earth stopped and there came the babble of thousands of tormented voices. The demons knew he was here. The curved sword blade ignited with blue fire surging from the end of it.

"Whoa'," Angus exclaimed, "it lives, the sword lives!"

140

The henge structure juddered again in front of him, its cut rocks crunching and grinding as if complaining about the wicked intrusion of the great demon army moving up through the tunnels below.

Angus knew this time would be the making of his bones. Yet still, basic human fear cut through him. Even so, the greater force of strength through the heavenly power cancelled it out. He didn't need any support now, for he was whole again, having been divinely prepared for his task through many interventions and rites of passage.

The ground around the Wheelhouse structure bounced up with a thud in an explosion of earth containing old plant roots, old bones, pottery and bits of iron. It was said that here had been the place where witches were brought to be buried. A sinister green mist hung in the air like a banner for the arrival of something far worse.

Then the first of the demons came up and out of the hole connected to the far away underground of Antarctica. A hundred or so of the lower demons were the first to emerge with their tools of war and torture created from petrified razor-sharp wood. They'd been pushed to the front as bodyguards of far worse beings. Angus had experienced these lowly class of demons accounting for at least a thousand of them with his Viking Sword, the Ulfberht. He watched them shape change into various humans like bogus media people. Their bodies were ugly and malformed. They aimed to inflict pain and suffering through any means. Angus disconnected the sword from its connector strip, and as he did it rolled itself up into the air dropping into the scabbard hanging off Angus's right hip. For the umbilical cord-like connector strip could never be lost, even if the Sword of Methuselah was destroyed by God, the only One capable of it.

Flooding out from the portal behind a thousand or so lowly demons were the distinctly more powerful lizard demons. They chose to use their lowly demons to do their dying for them, increasing their own power further by absorbing the suffering of these lowly servants. They scuttled out of the Wheelhouse like komodo dragons on all fours with their powerful muscular limbs. The stench that followed them was like burning sulphur. As one moved then so did they all as if they were joined together. They poured out of the portal with deadly purpose now standing like humans on two legs after their tails had shrunk up into their spines. They breathed out the bile known to erode most materials. Then, forming in a half circle, thousands of them now began to gulp in air, pumping themselves up like a spectacle of infernal bullfrogs. Together, like an exhibition from vile theatre, they projectile vomited their deadly green bile towards Angus, which slopped through the sky like turgid green paint in slow motion. Cohorts of lower demons raced towards Angus. The Methuselah Sword began to hum with magical power. As the lower demons surrounded Angus, he swooshed the sword back and forwards like he was cutting sugar cane. The lower demons were cut in half. As they came towards him, their dying flesh fell apart turning back into the faces of celebrities and then into scurrying insects which scuttled back to the demon army. Meanwhile, the green bile hung in the air above Angus like a frozen milk shake. After destroying the last of the lower demons, he looked up only to see bile falling from the sky towards him. He swung the sword of Methuselah against it. Before the bile got to him, the sword turned silver and fired out blue flames transforming it into jelly, saving him from a malevolent burning. The green substance fell in clumps onto the earth leaving cavities for him to avoid. A wailing of woeful disappointment rose from the higher demons marshalling the attack on Angus. Angus uttered a little prayer answered by the appearance of a bright light in the sky. He didn't have time to think about it as he jogged on in his pangolin armour, like a mad creature of the good. Angus charged the demon army, attempting to emerge from the Wheelhouse. They wailed woefully, knowing he carried their nemesis with the curved sickle sword of God's righteous power against them. Angus, the Grail Knight, engaged them. He appeared ever more menacing in his pangolin armour. It was an armour system created by Leonardo da Vinci himself working as God's great designer.

Angus scythed into the enemy and even Behemoth, their leader, backed away. Hundreds of demons fell dead with many retreating back. Angus flailed on, destroying all that stood in his way. Amongst the dead demons lay media personalities paid off by New Babylonians who had been 'soul sucked' on their way to the pit of everlasting fire. Behemoth rose amongst his minions, a toxic bastion towering above. Angus moved steadily slicing through all those who came near him with the sword bursting into flames every so often. The demons were losing ground. More and more gave way running back into the portal.

The bright light from the East grew in intensity. It was the sign that Angus should pay attention to. Just then he received a telepathic message from the light in the sky. *'Drive them back down into the shadows, seal off the portal and return to the Temple in London to join the Host of God as soon as possible'.*

Angus kept on with his relentless scything and slashing fluidly against Behemoth the demon leader. Angus walked over the lesser demons and indeed the higher ones to get to Behemoth who backed away standing on many of his kind, squashing them into green splodges of pulp. Angus pursued his prey lightly skipping over the demon bile pooling on the earth. He swished the demon slaying sword at its blubbering bulk, infested with sores and the faces of prominent New Babylonians. He could see Behemoth's frightened eyes as he continued against it. Every time Angus slashed Behemoth the green bile dripped from its cankerous skin. The bile which dripped onto Angus's jade armour rolled off like it was teflon. The demon army retreated in their thousands back into the tunnels under the Wheelhouse henge construction fleeing the awesome power of the sword. As Behemoth looked out of the portal Angus slashed across its face blinding it and cutting off its ear with searing accuracy. Backing off the demons and devils that came from the portal returned from where they came. Angus stood triumphantly looking down into the pit. Finally, a large boulder of stone flew through the air and plugged shut the portal hole silencing the screams of the 900,000 enemies of God which had tried to come onto the earth. But it was not finished, in fact, the battle had only just begun.

The voice returned to Angus. *"Wash your armour in the spring waters over on the plateau and then get ready to return to London. The demon army will be successful in its next attempt to enter Scotland. The people have betrayed me."* Angus looked around to find the supernatural voice.

"The demons will return through the Stroma fire festival." There was a pause. *"You have done well Angus, you have bought the necessary time to enable the Army of God to make it through the Temple portal. Go join your sisters and brothers."*

The spiralling light in the sky went out and Angus was left feeling cold in his pangolin armour. Exhausted he clunked over to the pool on the plateau before him. He walked in, drenching himself in its cold bracken waters. It was a place where the pure waters would null and void any poisonous effects of the demon bile residue. As he climbed out the other side, his armour came off by itself collapsing into a small case formed from the abalone helmet. Angus stood back aghast at how small it had reduced to. All was still, like frozen words. He was prompted to go down to the car park situated on the banks of Loch Eriboll. He knew that something from God would show itself to help him get to London. He'd done his job perfectly for once in his life. He slumped over in the rising morning sun. Curiously it warmed his bones nicely as he rested by the little tarn. He had no strength just yet to attempt the rigorous downward journey. But help was on its way.

Angus didn't have much time to contemplate the nature of the reality he was in. In fact, he'd previously accepted another version of that reality, much to his misfortune. He liked to call that the '*timeline of the elite*' because it seemed like it had been contrived to manipulate the working classes. He now knew where that was going. And then that version of time, without linear constraint, perforated his world. It came like multiple time sequences all strangely jumbled but making more sense than the linear version of events hammered out on some fake western calendar. He wondered if he tried with all his heart, he would be able to teleport himself. He wondered if he could think his way back to London. Still there was a nagging doubt. The New Babylonians had succeeded in making all the people doubt themselves. That way they continued to control the dumbed down masses, feeding them the crumbs from their toxic table. Yet Angus had broken that mould as recent events had proven. This had enabled him to fight the great demon army, yet even that now felt like a dream from a nightmare place. Or was he, in fact, in mid-episode of psychosis? It was time to find out!

Angus thought himself back to the Temple in London. He visualised gargoyles above the effigies of dead knights carved in stone. The knights lay with their legs twisted in various ways, exhibiting carved symbolism and body language, linking them to a clandestine sacred order of knights. Many of them were in the famous Tarot card illustration pose of the hanged man with its esoteric meaning. In fact, this order had been programmed to live in the reality of now, although they'd been designed for a particular purpose thousands of years ago, as Angus would learn. They were, in fact, a subculture of warriors, designed by the genius of God, before the onset of linear time. The New Babylonians had grown much worse than their progenitors, known simply as the Babylonians. These effigies in the Temple represented Grail Knights and just like Angus, they had been created for just such a time.

He imagined the knights back in the Temple again and again. He smelt the musty damp stone of the Temple all around. He noticed shadows inside the Temple formed by the sweeping movement of clouds scudding across London. He felt weightless sat on the Wheelhouse henge portal stones. And he began to taste the stone on which his head rested, which was compacted energy of millions of petrified sea creatures. Angus began to feel invigorated. Going deeper, he saw himself outside his body, sat looking into the mud above Loch Eriboll. He saw himself touching the Earth, feeling it, witnessing the soft glow of electric light around him. He summoned the portal again which appeared like a dark circular doorway rising above, borne up by a thousand miniature angels of light winging around it. He brought the light down to him, pointing his index finger and rolling it around, to bring about the magic to return him to London and *'The Battle For Reality'*.

The demon army flew, on accursed wings to the Stroma fire festival, through their unholy tunnels. Their intent was to return to the world, to inflict as much suffering on the people, whilst on their way to join those who had summoned them. Their purpose was to force the yoke of evil on humanity. In this new dimension they would be aided by artificial intelligence and the power of the Saturn Supercomputer, already brainwashing the masses. They'd already started sending humans to the recycling centres to re-use their good organs.

The only thing which had delayed the New Babylonians was the huge increase in giant rats which infested the recycling centres, try as they might it was impossible to destroy them. The rats kept reproducing progressively, in size and number, from feeding off the human waste. At one point the giant rats had gnawed through the armour-plated wiring of the Saturn Supercomputer itself, plunging the elites into total chaos for a few brief moments.

Angus thought himself deeper into the interior of the Temple in London. Then through some indescribable psychic unity with the molecular structure of stone Angus began to change into it, transferring into the form of his own effigy laying prostrate on the stone flags of the Temple. Now his effigy was back and lay along with the others in stone, waiting, watching. As he went back, he recited the sacred mantra, now for the first time. It was a magnifying verse from the immortal *'Book of the Stone Knights'*. He was finally remembering his source of power and his allegiances as a Grail Knight. As far back as biblical times he had made his bones as a Warrior Mason of Zerubbabel, those who rebuilt the second Temple and the great wall of protection around Jerusalem. Those whom we are told laboured with sword in one hand and trowel in the other, rebuilding the walls around Jerusalem.

As he went he recited the mantra out loud.

"I ride with those who watch in stone, those who wait the call. Rise before you fall. From stone to bone."

147

There was a flash and boom and the next thing he was in the Temple, gazing out of his stone effigy, bent legged and lying on the flagstones.

He saw his lips uttering the words as his effigy re-carved itself, complete with his segmented pangolin armour and abalone helm. For whatever Angus was or became then so did his effigy. There was a brief moment of silent blackness and peace. And then he lurched forward coming round to find the Temple full of the Army of God. Every square foot had been taken up by them in their war armour. They spilled out onto the surrounding streets to the misguided amusement of masked passers-by who stood and stared and pointed, making comments like, "Look, they must be filming about them Knights Templar, look at them, how white their robes are!" And more of, "I'll watch it myself, how splendid!"

More of the Brethren came out to prepare for the march on Westminster. That place once known as Parliament was now known as the House of Babylon and on the streets as 'the house of Liars'. It was difficult to discern if many of the passers-by were actually human and not artificial intelligence. It was getting ever more difficult to tell them apart.

The Pirate Brethren, who had been organising themselves inside, spilled out onto the streets brandishing cutlasses. Bemused lawyers above looked down from their chambers. They came out to watch, still wearing their pantomime robes and wigs adding to the spectacle. Then the familiar high-pitched sirens of the globalists' vans arrived to deal with what they thought was a disturbance on a film set. They were conditioned to go along with the myth of the media. Recently one in three of these operatives were now also artificial intelligence. Their most draconian looking Globalist Operatives came out of one of the vans. Pedestrians put on their masks. Most were already wearing them.

It was impossible for real life human beings to be in masks continually like the AI because of the health risks. London folk could only ever progress to becoming a Babylonian slave and the mask was a visual symbol of their compliance to being slaves; that couldn't be clearer.

As soon as the knights and pirates saw the globalist vans they retreated back from the streets, gathering in a shield wall outside the Temple's main doors. Red crosses on white mantles and shields clearly depicted who they were. Slowly they marched forward with their Templar Sergeants making up the flanks of the battle formation. For the moment Grand Master de Molay remained inside preparing the war host inside the Temple.

The Inner Sanctum Conclave

De Molay called an Inner Sanctum Conclave and all their forces stepped back, leaving a tiny circle of space for the seven Templar's of High Office to go about their business, including two of the Pirate Brethren. De Molay recited a prayer to Saint John the Baptist pointing to the Templar Scientist to take the floor. "Greetings my brothers and sisters I bring the news that we are ready to deploy the ant riders. Andrew Sinclair stands over near the High Altar ready with the High Priests of Aaron and the Holy Ark. We have a considerable force of the scorpion-tailed locusts and our ant rider allies have made the journey here with us". De Molay nodded from his hover chariot looking over at the twenty giant ants stooped down waiting for action ready to rise when required. They slumbered with the ant riders checking the armour of their mounts in preparation. The riders were careful not to touch their drooping feelers.

De Molay hovered down into the middle of the Conclave to preside over it. "And what have we from you Grand Marshal?" The Grand Marshal moved forward putting his right hand over his heart. "All is prepared Grand Master. The Templars and Sergeants will fight after their swords are changed into sonic weapons." De Molay looked pleased. "Well done, an incredible achievement to make our deadline. The enemy will not know of this development."

Outside, Globalist Officers stood back, exhibiting a brief admiration for whom they thought were actors. More globalists stomped out of the back of the van in riot gear, backing up the Globalist Officers who approached the Templar shield wall in riot formation, almost like they were competing with them. These were the same Globalist Officers who had forced the suffocating mask wearers on the Thames River walk to put their masks back on, assisting their deaths. These globalists had been handpicked for their adherence to 'small rule edicts', another part of the social engineering plan to subdue the people of Britain, turning them into slaves or prisoners. In the country of Hungary many years ago resistors to tyranny had turned on the agents of the people's oppression. The forces of oppression employed Hungarian traitors to enforce a lockdown of their own countryman. These traitors worked for a totalitarian regime 'coup d'état' and were paid in gold pieces as an incentive. However, many such traitors were discovered dead, sometimes with the gold pieces they'd been paid scattered over their bodies. No one would touch this gold, which was despised as tainted money.

The globalists moved closer as more were drafted in. Suddenly another Templar Marshal broke from the shield wall putting his sword back in its sheath and walking forward purposefully. The shield wall of Templars stood back in a more relaxed stance as he spoke.

"There is no need to take this battle onto the streets of London. Stand your operatives down and we can discuss what you have been living with. We ask not for terms, just for your understanding of the people."

"Throw down your arms and comply like everyone else and you will be spared," replied the Lead globalist still uncertain about the credibility of this new force raised against them.

More Templars stood ready behind the door as the emergency Conclave hammered out their war plan behind them. Knights were led by a Templar Commander presiding over every one hundred of them. Outside, events were escalating as more armed helicopters and drones appeared. Still the Globalist Force Operatives smirked, bemused at the situation as the emergency message to the Saturn Supercomputer had not yet got through to their units. Many globalists still thought they were watching a controlled television film production, nothing more than a promotion film of another medieval adventure.

The Zombie Signal

And then the inevitable happened. Suddenly all the mobile phones started to ring out flashing white light from their integrated torches. A million phones belted out a rhythmic emergency buzz which sent people first into panic mode and then into a compliant zombie like trance. The phones switched to emitting high levels of electromagnetic frequency radiation, just like the plastic trees now rooted on every road and shopping centre throughout the country; 'death sown by EMF'.

Hesitantly the Globalist Officers began to form up to march against the Templar shield wall. The people on the streets moved together like a flock of sheep to the emergency sorting shelters where they would be graded to be protected depending on their marked status. Those who had no marked status would be humanely dispatched and their body parts recycled.

The Templar Marshal had been briefed about what was happening. Anyone who acted independently or showed signs of non-compliance were identified and monitored by Artificial Intelligence. As the emergency signal stopped, one of the Templar Marshals picked up a standard loud hailer and barked down it, "All ye who do not comply, come here and we will give you shelter, act now to save yourselves!"

Some of the people halted in their tracks aware that their unmarked status would be discovered. One, then two and then more walked quickly to the Templars. It was surprising how many of them had indeed escaped as few turned to many, walking towards the Templars. "Save your souls from demonic tyranny; come to us!"

Globalists went into fight mode and jack-booted towards the Templar shield wall. Preparing to skirmish, they moved with the fake confidence of the visionless. Above, all was being monitored by artificial intelligence including the emotional responses of their own operatives, who had been brain chipped, which was an irrefutable precondition of their death cult allegiance. All Globalist Operatives were subject to conditioning which rendered them devoid of empathy towards humanity. More and more globalists formed up in the background. Drones hovered above like mechanical hornets relaying information and CCTV images, whilst below, forces of good and evil prepared for the biggest confrontation of ideology on British soil since the English revolution.

The Demon Army Emerges Through Fire

Angus had stopped the demon army from coming through the Loch Eriboll Wheelhouse portal with the Sword of Methuselah, buying precious time for the Army of God, so they could return through the portal in the Temple in London. But news was coming that the demon army were now emerging through the Viking fire festival, where its pagan nature had been a perfect portal for the demons. During this time people became sick and disillusioned and many folk lost their reason for living. More and more illness plagued the people wherever the demon army passed.

Many had blamed the recent draconian measures brought about by the elite New Babylonians. Meanwhile the demon army had increased in its own power through the misery and suffering it had inflicted on others. Suffering was their currency augmented by their lust for blood. But they had been stopped in their tracks by Angus and the flailing Sword of Methuselah.

Even though the demon army moved invisibly some folk could see it. Such people were declared as suffering from mass hallucination as would be expected from a governmental mechanism supporting incoming demons. But there were still folk in Gaelic Scotland who had the gift of the sight. Many of these could see the demons dancing in the flames and growing in power. The demons were as real as when Angus had fought them in the ice tunnels of Antarctica. And if their infernal leader's calculation succeeded then by the time they had reached London they would be at their most potent and their bile at its most dangerous, empowered by human suffering.

For the first time tourists and local people saw the flames flare up and grow in great intensity. Some of them had been singed and burned. The health service ambulances made their way to the scene with blue flashing lights. The huge green gas cloud rose up from the burning Viking ship. And the invading demon army made for the mainland. All was being prepared for their entry into London where they would be at maximum strength. The mass gathering of evil was intended as a display of abysmal force showcased in the New Babylonian capital. What they hadn't accounted for was the Army of God's arrival through the Temple Church portal. Only Agrimas, their Demon King was aware there would be further resistance.

The Demon King began to summon strange beasts from the nether regions of hell to help destroy all who stood in their way. He would be attended by the draconian globalist militia who had been slowly re-educated from their earlier lowly status as the enforcers of small rules and edicts. Many of them started as traffic wardens and were renamed as community dissent officers. And as their power over the people increased then so did the length of the peaks on their hats. Such persons were perfect to become globalist traitors. They were hand chosen for their blind compliance and hunger for power at any cost. They had served their time on the streets of London enforcing small rules, fining people who dropped litter and ticketing cars for parking offences. In time they began to enforce rules of non-compliance like not wearing masks in public or persecuting people entering zones out of bounds to the public. Such places included areas where surveillance cameras were being installed and where electromagnetic frequency fake trees were being positioned. They travelled a conveyor belt of corrupt power, from traffic warden to community enforcement officer, to non-compliance officer, to Globalist Strike Force Officer. Such women and men had also entered the ranks of the police subverting them to be the enemies of the public instead of their servants.

Back inside the Temple at the emergency Conclave, Jacques de Molay, the resurrected Grand Master of the Templars, was now advising his Templar Scientist in the Knight's Circle along with several higher officers from the Templar Inner Circle. The Templar Scientist had insisted on bringing a tank full of the scorpion-tailed giant locusts with him. De Molay had been unhappy about carrying any extra weight for their arduous journey through the Temple portal from the ice tunnels of Antarctica. But now he congratulated this knight for his convicted persistence.

"Well done my brother, we will need all the help we can get now."

"I did what needed to be done," replied the Templar Scientist bowing to his Grand Master. And by the way I took a liberty in bringing something else to the table, shall we say."

The Grand Master flashed an incredulous look, "what next my brother, what next?"

"Well, they've started to grow faster than I thought. I am not sure how large they will become." The Templar Scientist had been working hard on a new project developed from the essence of giant Chilean dragonflies. "I've put them at the front of the Temple. But I fear we will have to remove the Temple doors to release them."

The Grand Master switched the conversation to the locusts as he already knew their capability. The giant dragonflies had both shocked and surprised him.

"And I know the giant locusts will do their job accordingly. But please, we must deploy them wisely. We have the artificial intelligence trans-humans to account for and we do not know if their blood will attract the giant locusts. And now you tell me of giant dragonflies! Although I do concede, we will need all the help we can get."

As in past battles against the globalists, only the real human blood in their veins and that which ran without the essence of God would be targeted and petrified by the locust venom. Even those elites with new mechanical hearts complete with renewed valves and organs from the recycling plants would be fair game for the scorpion-tailed locusts. As long as some percentage of the anti-God human blood ran in their veins they could be slain.

Now the Globalist Force Officers began to press the Templar shield wall outside the main entrance of the Temple. The Knight Marshal backed off knowing he could do no more. The shield wall of white and red crosses parted and the Knight Marshal issued his order under duress.

"They will not listen to reason. Bring those that are non-compliant into safety. Then prepare to go to war!"

A cheer of glory rose into the air from the Host of God as the opposing Globalist Force Officers shuffled forward banging their shields with their batons. As yet, they were only prepared for a riot, like the many others happening over London and in cities and towns throughout the United Kingdom. But now, stood before the globalists, was the ultimate force of resistance against what had been termed the 'London mandates'. But what was really happening was a full-on takeover of London by the New Babylonian Globalists against the people. The mandates functioned contrary to the proper laws governing the people by the people. The New Babylonian laws were all pervasive and represented the great infamous change of leadership enabled by Britain's traitor leaders. But things were about to change.

Drifting unwittingly near the Globalist Officers, more of the homeless tent dwellers walked purposefully to the Temple's main entrance after learning about what was happening on the streets. As they shuffled past they were attacked by the Globalist Officers who beat them and thumped them to the ground. The Templar Marshal immediately issued the order for the knights to confront the globalists.

"Make way and fetch them into sanctuary, we will not let this happen; these are the new pilgrims, we must protect them."

The Templars moved forward drawing their swords. The two forces engaged and much to the surprise of the Globalist Officers, the Templars began to slash and stab them, some dropping dead instantly. The pavements glimmered with their pooling blood as it congealed like resin. The globalists then fired live rounds into the Templars, downing a handful.

"Forward Brethren, forward! Now is the time for the sonic swords," the Templar Marshal exclaimed with pleading hands to heaven. "Take these knights inside and bring in the non-compliant; we are here for them."

The shield wall parted and a rescue party, comprising of helpers and saved non-compliants rushed out, eager to help, carrying stretchers from behind the wall. Not all the people had gone over to the New Babylonians.

More new model AI Globalist Officers filled the empty spaces in the ranks, taking the places of their dead. As expected, they used deadly force against the knights, firing off live rounds which ricocheted off their bullet-proof shields. De Molay broke from the Emergency Conclave, hovering out bravely into the open streets, his mantle flapping showing its red Templar cross. He ducked, as a smart missile seared past him striking the Temple Church masonry and sending fragments scattering over the Templar resistors. Strangely, material spirit moved through the exploding fragments, rebuilding them and turning them around in the air. They fired back with catastrophic explosive force at the globalist army, who went down like skittled toy soldiers. The Templars moved forward, swords drawn at the ready. They were as silent as lambs ready to fight like ravenous lions.

From his hover chariot, de Molay launched multiple dart missiles at the drones, which exploded, falling in flames from the sky and spiralling down in broken plastic bits. As the battle for the streets around the Temple escalated more Globalist Officers surged into the area, still not aware of what was coming against them from inside the Temple Church.

The Templars had planned well. The bulk of the knights and pirates filed out through the small exit and lined the back streets, spiralling down the avenues of cloisters and lawyers' chambers like the living antidote to the real virus. Each Templar, sergeant or pirate moved silently knowing exactly where they were going. The Knights of Saint John had been kept back but were standing 'on guard' behind the main door. The magnificent ant riders talked soothingly to their giant war ants, formed up in a circle waiting for their battle stations. At the rear of the Temple Church, Andrew Sinclair waited patiently with the Ark of the Covenant and the Levi Priests. Behind them, transfixed in stone were the thirteen Grail Knights where Angus would take his rightful place.

Already the great tank of giant scorpion-tailed locusts was borne up and carried to the main doors ready to be released.

The battle commenced, quickly changing in nature as the Army of God enabled their swords to become sonic weapons. De Molay smiled as the Templar Scientist came out and switched their arms to use universal vibrational frequencies associated with the Earth's Schumann resonance. Despairingly, many homeless people and children were shot in front of the ranks of Templars in the shield wall. The Templar Marshal brought a mechanism known as a cosmic astrolabe. He twisted a few switches and cogs and it cranked into action. Soon the Templars were aiming their swords like rifles. They began to fire sonic waves at the Globalist Officers who dropped to the ground, disappearing into the stone flagstones, leaving only their death shadow staining the ground. The Templars fired devastating frequency beams from their swords at the Globalist Officers who had gunned down those non-compliant citizens attempting to cross over to the Sanctuary of the Temple. The shield wall juddered with purpose like a braking juggernaut. "Make ready Templars," was the cry as their shield wall stomped forward towards their enemy.

Still, the Globalist Officers and riot police streamed into the unfolding battle raging around the circular Temple Church now armed with extra sophisticated weapons. The conflict continued, whilst the main force of the Templars and pirates were filing out through the back doors of the Temple, into the London under-ground in smaller groups. Most citizens, in their zombified state, still thought they were watching a mock medieval pageant. The Templars and pirates made their way to the underground station like a stream of medieval actors. All manner of distraction raged in these final days to cover up the immense level of corruption and evil perpetrated against the people. The Army of God was aware of this.

Now the grizzled Soldiers of God sat in silence with their matted beards on the underground train, going to the place once known as Parliament. As usual, gang bangers were causing trouble on the underground. Public order was at an all-time low as it was designed to be, when suddenly the New Babylonians would announce their way to correct all wrongs, not just here but all over the world. Well-dressed thugs were getting on the train in an arrogant manner. Predictably, they started to make obscene comments about the Templars.

"There must be a show on in de' city, look at em' man. Strike him hard in de' face brother." This new breed of thug came from the streets and had been schooled in all manner of narcotic supply having been allowed to thrive without rectification, as the police service had been abolished. In its place there was a surveillance system that persecuted anyone doing good. People feeding the homeless, for instance, could be imprisoned and the key thrown away.

Lower humans in gold and silver tracksuits ruled the underground now. They were paid premium money through social media for posting violent or obscene videos which they created by carrying out acts of violence against random passengers. Indeed, it was a thriving business. It was common for decent folk to get punched or knocked out by the gangs roaming the underground and then videoed on mobile phones. Some of these violent film makers wore their own version of the standard masks customised with gang symbols. And some of them flashed their bar code marks set in their right hands or stamped on their foreheads like a saluting gang sign. These groups were acceptable amongst the emerging empire of Satan. 'Bad but compliant' was acceptable in this upside-down world. Some passengers tried to tough out the tension. Others got up scurrying down the train to the next carriage. The knights kept their vigil of silence. Then ignorant of the real nature of these warriors one of the gang bangers approached a knight and slapped him hard across the face. The Templar looked over at his commander who shook his head disapprovingly knowing what the Templar was capable of doing. The thug followed that up by spitting on him which the knight wiped from his face with his mantle without even a grimace. The blingers had made a mistake.

Although the commander's order was final with the knights it wasn't so with the pirates. There were thirty Pirate Brethren sat opposite the knights. The pirates were allowed to deal differently with the situation. The stench of old spice and rotting flesh should have been a warning to them. But not those damned by their own dumbed down senses. These gangs had been cultured on narcissism and low functioning morality and consequently they'd developed a lack of appreciation for the boundaries of real danger.

A tattooed pirate named Molineux acted first, drawing a long dagger and within an instant he'd cut off the ear of the gang member who had slapped and spat on the Templar. Blood spurted all over the plastic map of the London underground fixed on the carriage as the thug squealed. Confusion surged through the gang bangers as they fumbled for their weapons.

Meanwhile, Molineux exclaimed "Myn's an ear for a gold doubloon!" And all the Pirate Brethren cheered hurrahing. More underground users ran for the other carriages. Then a brawl took place at close quarters with a gang banger pulling out a 'Saturday night special' shooter unleashing mayhem. All the pirates got up and began stabbing and thrusting whilst stoically the Templars watched. Bloody screams were muffled over by the polite commands of the London

163

Underground female voice over the intercom. "Next stop Westminster. Please mind the doors." The pirates engaged with indigenous gangs, thrusting and cutting, slashing and bashing their way through them.

More pirates joined in, leaving the gang bangers ripped to shreds. They even politely sat the injured in the seats as they were leaving, some with missing ears, their shirts damp with blood. Another pirate even applied a tourniquet of leather around the leg of a girl who was bleeding out what was left of her life force. The first group of Templars and pirates left the train making for the steps out of the underground. As they went the Templars began to sing the prayer to the Lamb of God, a dedication to Saint John the Baptist, whilst the pirates sang out one of their anthems of blood and lost gold from South America.

As the Templars and pirates strode up the steps, other underground users in masks pushed back against the lime green ceramic tiled walls with trepidation. But their eyes twinkled above their masks with admiration. Many still thought they were in media Netflix land.

As the first underground train departed, the next cohort of knights and pirates got off the following train from the Temple, destined for the House of Babylon. At one point the Templar Marshal had stopped in front of an encampment of more unmasked homeless people. He addressed them, "Good people of London who have not complied with the tyranny, go to the Temple in London for your salvation, we will help you. Go whilst you can." Quickly more non-compliant people gathered their wits and started for the Temple dragging their rucksacks and trolleys away from their cardboard boxes and makeshift homes. Clearly now they were aware of what was happening. The battle for

London continued through both reality and in the dimension of the mind.

The Houses of New Babylon once known as Parliament rose up in the distance, restored in shiny white limestone and decorated with gold leaf. This building had once been the centre of democracy, or so many had been fooled into thinking. The force of knights and pirates approached these gates of opulence.

As the Templars went out onto the streets, another force of knights and pirates appeared at Westminster underground station, filing their way up and out to join them. One hundred at a time would follow, unaccounted for by the globalists who thought that they were witnessing another film production.

Where once that potent symbol of all that was British, 'Big Ben' had been, now three giant Babylonian gods facing out over Westminster resided. The sheets that covered the scaffolding had been removed to reveal Baal, Moloch and Nergal who stood like rectifiers of the old Britain of Peace and Sensibility. Many had expected to see a restored Parliament but what they saw, in reality, was the New Houses of New Babylon complete with Gates of Ishtar and all they stood for as corruption. And the people were in no state to object or put up any resistance. The Corporate state of Westminster was now completely devoid of any democratic value. And why should that matter? The average person didn't really care anyway. As long as they got their basic rations for complying, they were happy. As long as they could get their mind dumbed down on the telly and their array of both prescribed and un-prescribed drugs, they were fine. They lived on the conveyor belt of death, happy with their short-term thinking enshrined with materialistic delusion. In their minds, contentment was not about thinking for themselves. Happiness was being the slaves of New

Babylon. Yet others were forming up and sharing information and then organising themselves into small resistance groups against this new surge of infernal evil raging through London. People really were waking up.

Now the strange phenomenon of several hundred knights and pirates stood in battle formation outside the House of Babylon was happening. Many still thought it was just another costumed protest which would be quashed by the servants of New Babylon as quickly as any other. But more and more people were coming out of their hiding places enlivened by the idea of hope and another way of living.

Back at the Temple, the Grand Marshal and the Grand Master discussed the orders to be carried out and taken over to the Templar Scientist. They'd received intelligence regarding the approach of the demon army, currently on the borders of England and within an hour they would be in London. Controlled news outbreaks were broadcast from giant screens, recently installed all over the city, transmitting contrived pictures of a viral outbreak with plague-like symptoms such a large boils and sores and the threat of death. Hospitals had been closed for want of beds and many people lay dead on the streets. But what the people didn't know was that much of this fakery had been contrived to subvert the people and take over their societies.

Populations were making ready for another state of emergency health crisis. People double masked, covering their bodies in ridiculous plastic sheets. Media reports displayed people with giant wounds, crying children and parents sat in hospital in oxygen masks. More fear and destruction heaped like burning coals on the heads of the struggling citizens. Mobile phones began to flash a level two alert which meant people must return home. This was an order meant for only those who wore the orange masks of compliance chipped and registered through the Saturn Supercomputer. The masks carried a device that was instantly recognisable by those who had been marked as slaves. The non-compliant would be brutally dealt with. They would be caught and transported to the recycling units where they would be terminated and their organs harvested. What was left went as fertiliser for the new human meat farms. It was estimated that there were at least four hundred thousand people, half of which were homeless, that could be recycled by the New Babylonians; yet more profit!

Back at the Temple preparation for war was nearly finished; it was time for the Templars to unleash the rest of their secret army along with their secret weapons.

"They cometh brothers and sisters we will release the ant riders now! Take your positions the demon army is approaching, we have but one hour. They have reached the outskirts of the city." The Templar Marshal looked up at de Molay on his hover chariot. De Molay issued the 'war word' and the Templars went into their war plan.

De Molay issued the order for the ant riders to strike hard in Westminster. "Go and do your duty, take back the City!"

The twenty ant riders began to saddle their mounts after checking their armour. One by one they were led by reins to the rear door of the Temple church which they squeezed through carefully. Above them were the watching lawyers who had not chosen a side debating in their minds the best route forward. Some had been shocked at what they'd seen and had started to escape down into the tunnels of the Saturn Supercomputer to the safe compounds deep underground clearly made over to vast wrongness of what was happening. They scurried down the tunnels like cloaked ferrets running for their lives. It was clear a full-on attack was happening against the evil. As they went, de Molay fired more hypersonic dart missiles from his hover chariot above the Temple which exploded, scattering their papers and burning their furniture. A few other lawyers, who decided to serve the good and with the help of the Templars, grouped together and went down into the Temple from their chambers with pledges of loyalty to the Grand Master.

"We have done wrong by being impartial as the great evil was unleashed. Forgive us and let us work with you."

De Molay looked at them with his steel-like stare.

"We move as one, lawyer brothers and sisters. I invite you to begin proceedings against the New Babylonians. Go now and bring about your legal craft; invoke the Traitors Act and bring letters of high treason against them all!"

The lawyers nodded in agreement. "We shall have papers to you within the hour Grand Master."

The Grand Master turned his attention elsewhere nodding his approval whilst the giant ants with their feelers twitching were led through the rear door onto the street. They scented the air tasting it with their protruding mandibles. They too smelled the scent of the bad blood of the enemy as they opened their killer claws. They'd have no problem ripping through any metal armour protecting the New Babylonians like can openers. The ants could tear up and spit out any New Babylonian armour with ease. As their riders climbed on their mounts a contingent of Globalist Officers turned the corner into the street only to be met by the incredible sight of the giant ants.

The first fabulous ant and rider engaged the enemy, decimating their ranks by squirting poison from their abdomens at the Global Force Officers, melting them like wax toys. The ant rider patted the great ant head of his mount enthusiastically. They trotted on one after the other down the street and under the shadows of the Temple Church like a gothic horror tale. Following them were several Templar cavalry units, compromising of a cohort from the Knights of Saint John with their familiar black and white livery. Andrew Sinclair remained with the Priests of Aaron preparing the Holy Ark.

The Grand Master Proclaims

The enemy Saturn Supercomputer identified the threat and issued a full-on emergency. Globalist Force Officers were streaming into London from Greater London along with their civilian slaves, who'd sold out by conforming with 'The Acts of Compliance'. They'd been equipped with non-lethal weapons so that if any of them considered rebelling against their handlers they were essentially powerless. Slaves in their orange uniforms and masks were sent out in front, to take bullets and blades and anything else which might be levelled at the security forces. Many of the non-compliant joined the Templars and the pirates as auxiliaries, helping in any way they could, particularly as stretcher bearers. Those who had military experience were knighted and brought into the fold as penitent knights. They were armed and went willingly into the battle.

Overhead de Molay had left the Temple and was seen speeding through the air dodging enemy drones in his ether hover chariot. Andrew Sinclair had been left in charge of the rear-guard forces, which included firing up the Holy Ark. The last Grand Master of the Knights Templar began to descend down on what had once been Parliament, now protected by the Gates of Ishtar. As de Molay floated downward through the haze, the ant riders appeared, lurching onwards to join the main bulk of the Army of God, who were waiting, grouped in battle formation outside Westminster tube station. Now they were changing their weapon's, setting to sonic destruct. The force field around de Molay deflected enemy drone missiles, which exploded outside the iron railings of what is now known as the Houses of New Babylon. Yet de Molay descended to the ground to read out 'The Proclamation', issuing proceedings against the traitors of Britain.

From the streets and alleys hundreds of Globalist Force Officers came marching and jumping out of riot vehicles. It was the biggest show of force London had ever seen. Multiple television screens around the capital had been commandeered to transmit de Molay's speech to the people of London. People cheered happily for the first time since the New Babylonian power system had been installed.

"I need no introduction, no courtly rules here, ye worshippers of false gods and Mammon. You, who have falsely claimed to steer this nation for the people and you have betrayed every facet of democracy here, and so in the world. It is clear you are working with the dark forces as you've done from day one. I told you that one day there would be an accounting for your actions and this day will be it. I am issuing proceedings against all of you under the Traitors' Act for High Treason! The regime you represent casts you as the enemy of God and that is why we have returned."

Cheers rose up into the air from the people; a cheer that was most welcome in the turbulent activity that was around. People who watched the screens could not hold themselves back. The giant ants with their riders went into action attacking the globalist force vans, mangling them and throwing them into the air still packed with officers. Only one ant was brought down crumpling on the sidewalk after an enemy dart scorched it between the eyes.

The Templar formation, comprising of one thousand knights and sergeants sprang into action, stooping low into battle mode and moving forward towards the Houses of New Babylon. The Pirate Brethren had gone into a full attack, with their fittest combatants climbing over the railings with elasticated ropes and scaling ladders. They engaged with security staff in hand-to-hand combat. The battle raged inconclusively. Although better and stronger the Pirate Brethren were fewer in numbers.

The non-complaint had organised themselves into a partisan army with a makeshift flag bearing the hand of God. It was clear they'd been planning their move. Although weak in the flesh they were strong in spirit and moved forward slowly yet purposely against the enemy, huddling close together as much for comfort, as from fear.

Templar cavalry thundered down the streets as if from some other age, protected within a barrier of blue universal light. But more Globalist Force Officers piled into Westminster as the full emergency was announced. Many of them were part human, functioning with the remnants of real blood combined with a synthetic version, just like the AI in the Gorgon's Head pub. But the dreaded giant locusts were being readied for release. They could detect the bad blood, that blood in an altered state changed by man yet inspired by demons.

172

The Arrival of the First Wave of the Demon Army

Now the demons were here. Unfortunately, their putrid green gasses had been seen on the outskirts of London. With it came various illnesses starting with people succumbing to ancient plagues and unknown maladies. As the giant ants and their riders crunched their way through the enemy, the demon army flooded in, surging up through every tube and dark subterranean passage there was. The lower demons were the first to appear. There were still a few hundred or so left and Agrimas, their King, had forced them to the front to test the waters as had happened in the ice tunnels. As was their nature they attacked vulnerable persons on the street first. The toxic demon gas which acted as a smoke screen evaporated and they became visible, as the cobbled together bits of monsters they were. Breaking railings to use as weapons, the street people began to fight back. In fact, they began to use anything they could to fight with as they walked bravely forward. They suffered great losses but their courage more than compensated for their lack of commitment to the proper cause. Fearfully, they approached the demons. On seeing the brave resistance from the people, the Templars sent two hundred knights across to Westminster Abbey to help them. These knights were protected from the demon bile by angel gossamer silk that they wore under their armour. Demons engaged with the Templars like rabid beasts. They brought out their knives and killing irons attacking the Templars in multiple waves. But the Templars remained defiant and sang battle hymns as they stabbed and fired back at them with sonic weapons, slaying many demons, leaving them squirming on the ground like chopped slugs. And as in the ice tunnels, the demons were eviscerated, leaving only a shadow of their previous human forms. The sad element to this was that the demons had once been living breathing human beings, like bankers, teachers, politicians; everyday folk who had given up doing good, to do bad, in order to survive in the system of the beast. These people had hungered for power and had sold out their families to evil and those who lust to take God's position. Now they lay there on the pavements of London like the bleached out soulless images they had become.

Meanwhile the brave resistors fell in behind the shield wall of Templar might. The lower demons gave ground under the pressure, but then they'd only been submitted to the battle as cannon fodder anyway. After being beaten, their exploding bodies wetted the sidewalks and pavements with green blood. But something far worse was following, rising from the toxic green gas remaining in the sewers, culverts and dark places under London. At first, the gas hung like devil's mist above the filthy sewage of London, used as dabbling ponds by the giant rats.

The Lizard Demons Attack

These new demons took the form of monstrous reptiles, like lizards and deformed snakes and chameleons. One of their kind stood out from the rest as their leader. It was not large or powerful or even frightening to look at, but never was there a more malignant creature in the history of abominations. It was a basilisk, the most potently dangerous reptile hybrid known. It was a small misshapen creature, with a tail and a membranous fin, incarnated in the form of an abysmal cockerel-lizard hybrid. Its teeth were blunt crunchers designed to bite through both bone and metal. Its tongue was barbed and laced with poison and its look alone could kill. It was accompanied by its abhorrent offspring. This was a reptile whose bite was so poisonous that nothing was thought to be able to overcome its power. It would kill for the sake of killing once its morbid death stare locked onto its victim. The basilisk led its noxious family out of the tunnels onto the pavement, melting everything in their shadow. Out of the green vitriolic gas the other demons and reptiles manifested as real flesh, and scurried up and out from the London sewers, attacking the Army of God. This was the second wave of destruction. De Molay was now safely positioned high above Westminster, observing the invading demons in the form of reptiles and snakes, sent to soften up the Templars. De Molay sent an order to the Temple to finally release the sacred beasts which had waited through time, carved in stone as gargoyles. These good beasts combined different animal forms like jaguars and lions with eagles and falcons. Along with them were griffins and condors and all manner of small animals now transformed from stone to flesh, from hard rock to soft living flesh, with their sinews enlivened with the breath of God. They strained, cracking from their stone prisons and gathered together under the direction of an invisible angel. As the angel descended from the heavenly realm, the sacred beasts watched, looking up expectantly like sheep after their shepherd. With a soft voice it issued the order '*infecto negotio*' which meant 'unfinished bad business'. The message was conveyed so that the sacred animals would be released from their obligations, able to return back to nature on completion of their final penance to God. They waited, grunting, screeching and roaring, pawing the flagstones outside the Temple ready to go to the battle.

"Go to war my children, it is time," de Molay exclaimed from above.

And the sacred beasts charged and thundered towards their reptile adversaries, who had started to grab and tear at the non-compliant people, picking them up and running down the streets of Westminster with them hanging from their mouths, devouring them and feasting on their flesh, sending shock waves of horror to the others. People were seeing the truth of their situation.

De Molay threw his hands in the air as the sacred creatures charged after the monstrous reptiles. A deadly thrashing of paws, and skittering claws went down the mews and side streets, buffeting into the Lizards with a rending and tearing of flesh and limbs. Stood waiting in shadows, the basilisk family weighed up their enemy and then attacked the smaller animals like badgers and stoats, turning them inside out with their poisonous breath until their hearts stopped and they thudded to the floor. De Molay watched above holding his head in his hands. More good sacred beasts joined the fray, catching the reptiles and devouring them. The basilisk retreated only to appear further up the street to attack condors and eagles before they were able to lift off the ground. Many sacred beasts of God also lay dead or dying on the streets of London. But more flew in from other churches from near and far to help their kind.

Weasel Warriors

Above the battle, de Molay received a message from the Temple. The message was an apology from the Templar Scientist.

"Grand Master forgive me, I have forgotten to release the weasels and they are the only creature capable of killing the basilisks, the only one known to man. And in the past they have been the symbolic body guard, in a literal sense, to our Lord Jesus Christ."

"Please just do it Templar Scientist, we need them urgently."

De Molay was patient, for everyone was under terrible strain. Filing along the ground, a group of weasels emerged from the drainage culverts, having been summoned from church gardens where they lived in the walls. They spied the basilisk family, scuttling over to engage the forces of good. As soon as the basilisks saw the weasels, they stopped dead in their tracks, forming a protective ring around their horrible guardian. But the weasels moved into action engaging with the basilisks who cowered protectively together against their dedicated enemies. The weasel's Holy Scent protected them as they engaged the basilisks fearlessly. The basilisks moaned in terror knowing what this fearless friend of Christ was capable of. With all its might the parent basilisk focussed its deathly glare on the weasels that moved closer. The attack of the weasels began and they bit the basilisks, turning them over like miniature wrestlers rolling over and looking for the throat for blood. More weasels swarmed in from the gardens and walls of old London churches attacking the basilisk leader ferociously. For now, the power of this ugly creature was contained by the weasels, but something else was running through the sewers of London, ready to make a move in the changing power zones of the 'Battle for Reality'.

Back at the Houses of Babylon, once known as Parliament, the Pirate Brethren were fighting to open the gates. Disastrously for them though, the gates had been reinforced in preparation for expected attacks by those who dare to resist.

Above, de Molay had seen them struggling to open the gates for the Forces of God who were amassing outside, singing anthems of the good.

"Order one of the giant ant riders to assist them; our pirates are struggling to get in!" Immediately, a giant ant and rider broke from the group battling the Globalist Officers at the underground station of Westminster and lumbered over towards the gates of the Houses of Babylon. The ant rider urged it to charge at the gates. The pirates stood back as the giant ant lurched forward grasping the iron railings with its mandibles and started to twist them. The gates cracked and strained as it rived them apart. The reinforced stone gateposts exploded with bursting masonry as the gates were ripped clear and thrown into the air like scrap metal. Even whilst still in the air, the Pirate Brethren were already charging for the main halls of the New Babylon, armed with all manner of weapons. They were on a mission to capture one of the main leaders, a woman who had once been Prime Minister, but was now called the Supreme Accountant. This Globalist Leader was the equal in terms of power to the King of the Demons, Agrimas. Like many leaders of this regime, she was completely unaccountable. In fact, globalist ranks of power described the exact opposite of what their holders were supposed to do in reality. Everything in New Babylon worked in reverse and purposefully to subvert, twist, or make upside down. It tried to put their gods from below above all others including the one and only God.

De Molay swooped down from above urging the Pirate Brethren on to find the Supreme Accountant, for she had been consorting with the demons and had brought them in against the people. The Pirate Brethren surged through the gates followed by de Molay hovering behind them. As they entered over the smashed gates, the second wave of demon beasts appeared and rushed towards them. They were more furious than ever and certainly more ruthless than the first wave of lower demons, now mostly destroyed by the Army of God. These demon beasts had been made in hellfire from the remains of the most evil regimes seen on the Earth since Biblical times. They were working directly for their Demon King, Agrimas who lumbered behind them urging them on. The green mist cleared and on seeing the Pirate Brethren running through the gates, they changed direction swirling together towards them.

The Knights of Saint John of Jerusalem appeared ready to charge again. Their horses whinnied with expectation, hoofing at the stone pavements. The order was given and they charged, thundering against the new batch of demons who were attempting to relieve the pressure being forced on the security staff at the gates of New Babylon by the Pirate Brethren. Laura Bellamy was crawling along the tarmac followed by her finest pirate crew. On seeing this progress the Templars blocked the gate entrance to stop the reptile demons from following.

Scorpion-Tailed Locusts

De Molay swooshed back to the Temple to marshal the rest of the forces on their way over ground. He ordered the Templar Scientist to release the giant locusts. The Templar Scientist promptly went over to the large tank in which they'd been brought from the other place; that kingdom where the City of Light was.

"Yes, Grand Master I am doing it now. We are late, this should have been done sooner!"

He cranked the handle on the outside of the tank. The glass roof rolled back and the giant locusts, with their sticky foot pads climbed out of it and waited. The Templar Scientist timed the event on his magic amulet, counting down to their release. Oddly all the locusts focussed their beady eyes on something inside the Templar church. They were programmed to only destroy beings with blood that was changed, being contrary to the laws of God. With a worried look the Templar Scientist released them into the church as a huge swarm. They circled round the inside of the Temple like miniature motorbike riders and instead of making for the open rear doors, as the Army of God had done when it marched out and down the streets, the giant locusts landed by a second lower altar near those doors. There was a commotion and then the locusts lifted up together again and exited, with a whirring of their wings out onto the streets. Confused, the Templar Scientist walked over to find a dead crow. On further examination he realised that it was an AI version, with mechanical wings and a lithium battery heart pump, but there were drops of blood around its beak, and its chipped components melted before his eyes. It dawned on the Templar Scientist that this AI crow had been sent to watch the Army of God in the Temple. But there was some element of real life left in it, although its blood had been changed to flow through

AI mechanisms invented by the New Babylonians. The DNA of its blood had been meddled with and that was why it had been stung to death by the giant locusts. The Templar Scientist grimaced sending on the information to Grand Master de Molay.

Andrew Sinclair sat in silence with the Priests of the Holy Ark who were away from the battle preparing. He was in deep prayer and preparation for the final battle and could not under any circumstances be disturbed. A low light was beginning to emanate forth from the Holy Ark itself. As the praying team of Levi Priests prayed, then slowly, the Light from the Ark increased.

Meanwhile, the super locusts, with their humming wings went flailing through the air. Sensing and scenting the bad blood below them, they started to attack random Globalist Force Officers. Soon many of them fell to the floor with some of the giant locusts still attached to them. Once they'd withdrawn their scorpion-tailed sting, they attacked any one they could whose blood scent was profane.

Yet more Globalist Officers appeared, like a seemingly endless supply coming from everywhere. Agrimas, now put his despicable battle plan into action. Many more humans who'd consented to the evil plan of the New Babylonians lined up in front of the Demon King. They were brought into the battle after first losing their souls to the surrounding demons. Changed in some infernal way, they began to develop into a subspecies of part demon and part human. They quickly joined the battle bringing unbearable consequences against the good. The weight of these new numbers began to tip the scales in favour of the New Babylonians. Knights fell and were quickly dragged away to be butchered by the demons. Even the weasels began to retreat, forced backwards by the now emboldened basilisk and its damned children.

De Molay began to despair in this quickly changing battle arena. He had just not anticipated some of the moves made by the enemy.

Then King Agrimas reached out, catching a giant ant by its hind leg. It seemed powerless to resist his incredible strength. Agrimas dwarfed all around him. He bit the head off the giant ant flinging its rider through the air who landed skewered on the iron railings of the House of Babylon. A welter of blood splashed over the Pirate Brethren nearby. Agrimas then wrapped up the broken ant body with ease like old newspaper, bashing it into a bundle. But the incredible locusts were coming now, their wings buzzing down the streets as they descended in a deadly cloud to attack the demons. Agrimas swatted them away but other reptile demons suffered their deadly stings, dying instantly, their fake blood freezing in their veins. The locusts bought more time, but they were not enough to stop the self-replicating demonic forces testing the Templars. In the heat of the battle, Laura Bellamy and her pirates had made it through to the main doors of the House of Babylon. By some strange chance the Supreme Accountant was still in the building, but Laura and her team were closing in. During the intense fighting the Supreme Accountant lost contact with her security, who had been killed by the Pirate Brethren. The locust swarm entered through an open window into the House of Babylon. There was no stopping them as they wiped out every living or dead thing sustained by their unholy blood.

The Supreme Accountant ran from pillar to post, looking for a way out. She was, in fact, responsible for both impoverishing and attacking those she was supposed to be looking after. All around the battle raged with blood running down the streets. On seeing how little progress against them had taken place, de Molay gave permission to the

Templar Scientist to release his secret weapon. As the bodies piled up on the streets of London, de Molay was becoming desperate.

"If we've anything left to bring in, now is the time; we are losing too many knights and the non-compliant are being slaughtered without remission."

"I already took the liberty of releasing it. I heard what was happening and couldn't get in touch with you." The Templar Scientist had already gone too far, risking much by his actions.

"Ok, do not worry, we need all the help we can muster over here."

"If I am not mistaken our asset should be with you now."

The Dragonfly

De Molay was grateful, for even he was beginning to lose heart. As he stooped down again in prayer a huge shadow appeared above. At first the Grand Master covered his head with his mantle, for even he could not bear the thought of what it might be. Well, it was here, and its shadow darkened the streets below.

"Grand Master, I rather miscalculated the dragonfly eggs. It has grown incredibly fast and we had to recall one of the ants to take off the Temple doors so that it could emerge."

"My God, my brother, what have you done?"

As they talked, the monster dragonfly passed over de Molay casting a strangely cross-like shadow. The demons started to stop their horrific actions sensing a new threat entering the battle. Folding its transparent wings, the gargantuan dragonfly landed on top of a utilities building opposite the Houses of New Babylon. Then, like it had been switched on to the evil around it went into action, hovering down with its glimmering wings and bug eyes refracting light. It lifted swathes of demons in great scoops off the ground, crushing them to pulp with its immense jaws.

"Woah!" shouted de Molay, "it is in fact a tool for the good!"

"Yes, it is Grand Master, I worked long and hard to create it," replied the Templar Scientist.

As the huge dragonfly caught the demons in all shapes and sizes, another problem against the Army of God was happening. For out of every orifice of the stones and drains of the streets of London, there appeared supersized rats. Those demons that fell back to a rear position after the onslaught of the dragonfly were now faced with giant vociferous rodents whose need for meat knew no bounds. Meat to them was anything, dead or alive. And they'd grown, remaining immune to the effects of the bad blood of those marked who'd gone over to the Saturn Supercomputer, which was coordinating the dreadful events taking place.

Word had been relayed to the Grand Master that the Saturn Supercomputer had the ability to move from place to place in some way like a giant hydra.

Dragonflies have always been known to bring change in a spiritual sense and indeed this one was bringing better fortune to the Army of God, which had been struggling. Agrimas skulked out of the way and plotted, watching the huge dragonfly consume his demon army like a combine harvester with a mouth of metal teeth. Then a bolt of ugly green light hit the Demon King. It was a de facto communication directly from the Saturn Supercomputer itself, which had now become sentient, for the Saturn Supercomputer lived.

Agrimas, King of the Demon Army summoned his fearsome priests of death. They arrived after his incantation to the blood of devils. His eyes rolled over and he mumbled incoherently. It was the incantation spoken by his witches that brought about a huge change in the atmosphere. They had the ability to manipulate the membrane of time between planes of energy, known also as dimensions. As the witches mumbled their hideous incantation, the Saturn Supercomputer, which had been confined to technological parameters, began to change through waves of vibrating darkness and light.

This monster computer was changing into flesh in some unfathomable way. As of yet, it had only been able to move about on tracks and bogies under London in a secondary subway system, where it could function as a weapon against both flesh and material. It was also responsible for sending out depression and illness and even death against populations, through manipulation of electro-magnetic brain waves. Now Agrimas was sacrificing himself and his wicked life force so that he could enter the Saturn AI unit, augmenting its already horrendous power. In this cocktail of evil transmutation, a new form of fake flesh was beginning to appear. Waves of tangible energy vibrated throughout Westminster as it began to form into a dark entity of flesh, which appeared to live, spliced with technological advancements of microchipped technology. Thousands of non-compliant people from the streets of London now ran to the Temple, whilst the compliants bowed down in their masks and worshipped this emerging God of the Underworld.

All sacred beasts on the side of the good gathered together and moved away from the unfolding spectacle, waiting expectantly for a new opportunity to attack their enemy.

Now fortified with the demon soul of King Agrimas and the Saturn Supercomputer, this evil hybrid developed into form, not seen on Earth since the early battles between the angelic hosts. Those battles between the rebel angels and the Angels of God led by Saint Michael the mighty. Slowly but surely the Saturn Supercomputer changed, imbued in some way by Agrimas. And so it turned into a dark winged menace of rancid matter. Around him, the once deadly scorpion-tailed giant locusts had fallen over, legs twitching in the air and were dying off. Something infernal was doing its deadly work against the Forces of Good.

The Grand Master is Hit

De Molay looked down in dismay. And then, from some unknown angle, a dart missile hit his hover chariot and it puffed to the ground with yellow smoke belching from its power pack. De Molay survived. Even though he was partially disabled by his past battle wounds, he climbed out and hid under the cover of an arch of a tiny church known as the Little Gem. It was the perfect place for now. He waited, checking his communication system to the Temple. Strangely, the carving on the keystone above him was of King Solomon holding a key. De Molay knew he had but one chance left as the blood of his knights ran down the gutters of Westminster. But not all was lost. Many knights had escaped the explosion from the transmutation of King Agrimas and the Saturn Supercomputer and started to regroup. All that remained of the body of the Demon King was an over blown sack of flesh that had already

186

started to decompose, but it was nothing more than a biological sleeve which had housed extreme evil.

The dragonfly, meanwhile, had gone into a catatonic state, waiting on top of the utilities building opposite the House of Babylon. The weasels had backed off from the horrible leader of the second wave of reptile demons, as the war events between good and evil had taken a turn for the worse against the good. The forces of good and evil had backed away uneasily from each other in anticipation of a final conflict.

Only the Pirate Brethren continued to hunt for the Supreme Accountant of Britain, unaware of the change of events outside. Now something was happening inside the Houses of Babylon as small explosions lit up its windows. Then a woman emerged from a central doorway. She ran towards a side exit, pursued by the spectacle of pirates brandishing cutlasses and lead by Laura Bellamy. It was a scene of hope in the pantomime of despair.

De Molay used an emergency contact system, sending a watch number code to the Templar Scientist back at the Temple. He then reached for side arms as the demon army lumbered into action. But this time they were led by the dark shadow of the fallen angel, flashing with barcodes and negative energy and noxious blood, which offended all that remained of the good. All the time its negative power increased seven-fold, as surveillance information and barcodes filled its dark holes with the essence of those that now worshipped it and had been marked by barcodes. This was the final part of the plan to create a technological entity combining great evil with advanced technology called Artificial Intelligence. Yet it was dead; it was a dead thing with fake flesh and flashing lights substituting for a soul.

The huge plague of rats waited, piled on top of each other in suspended animation and fixed by the fear of what was happening around them.

Gregorian Chant 667

Over at the Temple and on receiving the emergency numbers 667 from de Molay, the rather eccentric Templar Scientist read out the final order.

"Oh my, this really is the end game, how should I do this? My voice is not good anymore, not good at all!"

The key to the numbers must be sung out like a Gregorian chant as this format repelled demonic energy. He began to sing the sacred chant, rhyming the numbers "667 667 667 667".

From the stillness in the rear of the Temple, Andrew Sinclair got up. He was trembling slightly. And it was as if the Ark was "connected to him by an invisible thread. The Holy Ark levitated from the flagstones of the Temple. Mumbling ominously and looking behind him, he muttered, "I was afraid of this. Now it won't be long before Angus wakes again. It's our last chance. We have nothing else left."

The Grail Knights Awaken

The Templar Scientist continued to chant out the numbers 667 over and over in Gregorian chant form. Finally, something began to stir. Although his voice seemed awkward and out of key, soon he was chanting like a seasoned Cistercian monk. The numbers he was reciting were invigorating the stones of the Temple and also the effigies of the Grail Knights including Angus MacWilliam. With them were the famous Marshal Knights and their bodyguards. In total, including Angus, their number was thirteen.

Angus's effigy held the Sword of Methuselah as it slowly began to move, vibrating in time with the Gregorian chanting from the Templar Scientist. Angus was the first to rise out of his stone chrysalis. Cracks appeared on all the effigies as the pure light of God shone through them. The Grail, which had returned to enable Angus's travelling between dimensions, opened with white light and with so much energy the remaining crows in the Temple eves above, flapped their black handkerchief wings out into the streets around. Now the whole of the Temple pulsated with gleaming radiance.

Angus lived again! Sitting up as stone, he cracked into real living flesh as did the other Grail Knights. One of them would assume command. The greatest knight of all, Sir William Marshal took control. Marshal was their most senior knight and tried and tested in battle. In the background, the Templar Scientist continued to chant. Images of the number 667 floated around like a numerological hologram, illuminating the alchemical process, which enabled stone to become living flesh. Andrew Sinclair even saw the numbers coming into focus all around the Holy Ark and in a childlike way, tried to grab them. The solemn Levi Priests stood behind the floating Ark as it began to move in the direction of the Temple entrance. Andrew Sinclair rose and followed them. As they advanced out, they were joined by the Grail Knights in the process of metamorphosis between stone and flesh. Sir William Marshal gave the order for battle, needing to be ready for all eventualities. They marched through the streets like an impregnable fortress nearing Westminster. This wedge of stone knights was now engaged on a supernatural mission. The Saturn Supercomputer had become a fallen angel and was the first thing to recognise the danger of the Grail Knights. Saturn sat there contemplating its next evil move as it pulsated with bar codes.

One third of the demon army lay dead, putrefying rapidly on the streets around, attracting more rats to feast on them. Many Templar Knights also lay dead. King Agrimas of the Demons became reanimated inside the fallen angel of Saturn, combined with the mordant energy of microchipped necromancy.

As the thirteen Grail Knights approached the enemy, the reptile demons moaned and wailed again, knowing that the Sword of Methuselah was coming for them. The Grail Knights were now well placed to help. Sir William Marshal barked out the first order of the day as the demon beasts formed up ready to attack. One brave weasel, a beloved creature of Christ, attacked the basilisk inflicting a bite on its neck from which it could never recover. Its green blood spurted out and more weasels joined in against it. For only the weasel in the dynasties of animals was immune from the poisonous blood of the basilisk. This was the sign for the forces of good to re-engage. A bright light shone out above London.

"Sir Angus MacWilliam, prepare yourself man! Bring out the Sword of Methuselah." Angus came forward with his hand grasping its bone handle, whilst it remained sheathed. Shadows picked out the details of Angus's pangolin armour flickering around its segmented form. There were moments when their 'stoneness' oscillated between living and inert matter as the knights became pure flesh. Sir Richardson and Sir Palin, bodyguards to Sir William Marshal, broke ranks and went over to where de Molay was hiding under the keystone of the Little Gem. They escorted him back into the wedge of knights, directing him into the middle where he would be protected. De Molay brought out his sonic sword in readiness. And forward they marched, singing the lost and sacred hymn to Saint John the Baptist, increasing their protection seven-fold against the menace of the Saturn fallen angel.

"All other knights make ready for battle. This is our time, spare none of them."

The Grail Knights marched forward in wedge formation led by Sir William Marshal with Angus MacWilliam at his right side. The demons, led by the Saturn entity, recognised the Sword of Methuselah and were already planning their next move. For they intended to both escape the sword's wrath and re-forge the demon army against it. The Grail Knights, however, were protected by their ability to fluctuate between stone and flesh.

The Demon Army Infests London's Rats

Meanwhile the Saturn entity coerced the remaining demons to go into the rats to protect them so that they could attack the threat of the Grail Knights. It was an unexpected opportunistic manoeuvre. The hated Saturn fallen angel boomed out its wicked orders at them. The demons transmuted into a pungent green mist like the essence of coffin liquor and infested the rats, going into them like a hand into a glove.

During this time, the remaining Templars formed backup and looked for other brothers and other forms of the good lost on the streets near the Houses of Babylon. They were followed by what remained of the sacred beasts of the good. The giant dragonfly began to wake, as though switched back on and a few of the remaining scorpion-tailed locusts joined it. Like an airborne bodyguard from above, they skittered down to pick off the servants of the Saturn entity, both stinging and dismembering them to death.

Still unaware of the reality outside, Laura Bellamy could be seen chasing after the Supreme Accountant of Britain through the Houses of Babylon. The Supreme Accountant stumbled and Laura Bellamy grabbed her hair and after dropping her cutlass Laura Bellamy slapped her greedy face.

"If you want to keep your miserable life even in the short term you shall be tested by a court of the people in the Temple!" she exclaimed. A look of sheer terror flashed over the Supreme Accountant's face. It was like she'd awoken from some dark dream where she'd been the despot against the people. She had been responsible, under the influence of demons, for subverting the police, turning them into Globalist Strike Force Officers against the people. Yet the truth was, Laura Bellamy could see the line of her evil extending right back to

South America. Many Nazis had been captured by the Pirate Brethren and the Nazis had learned of their connection to the Babylonian families who were holding the world to ransom. Somehow, their evil persisted within the plan for world domination.

After witnessing the capture of the Supreme Accountant, also known as the Whore of Babylon, the Saturn entity directed the giant rats against the Army of God. The rat swarm consisted of over a million of their kind, led by gargantuan versions. They had been the cause of so much trouble against both marked and unmarked people of London. They scurried and squirmed towards the Houses of Babylon, just as the wedge of Grail Knights came into focus, standing directly in front of them. Although the rat swarm appeared organic enough, it was imbued with the caustic spiritual energy of the demon army. Green mist followed in their wake, laced with disease and other putrid viruses.

Angus MacWilliam grimaced under his abalone shell helmet. He unsheathed the Sword of Methuselah which crackled and sparkled with micro lightning bolts. Nevertheless, the rats came on to devour the enemies of the Supreme Accountant, who was really the Whore of Babylon responsible for crushing the will of the people for the New Babylonians.

They swarmed around the wedge, but stopped dead in their tracks, frozen with fear as Angus stepped in their way. De Molay brushed off many rats which had attached themselves to Angus's pangolin armour. He need not fear them; nothing evil could penetrate the angel gossamer worn under his armour. Then micro lightning bolts burst their bodies, like bags of blood, scattering their guts into the air and leaving splatters against the walls of London like modern art. Angus started to scythe into them, swinging his curved sword and chopping into the wall of rats before him. As he cut at them, the wriggling wall of rats grew in height, endeavouring to climb over him. Sometimes, the negative electric energy of rat flesh failed and horrific demons that had been disguised in rat-form became visible. But they were nothing more than a vitriolic virus engineered to look more terrifying than they actually were. This became clearer as their demon spirit form expressed the real horrors of their eternal sufferings. Their contorted grimacing faces reflected every bribe and every sin they had ever committed against the innocent, played over and over again in eternity. Only at the point of physical death does a person know what comes next in their afterlife; many would learn that *'not every sin in this world goes unpunished'*.

At one time, these creatures had been ordinary humans, like people of the establishment who had sold out their values and opted to be in the pay of their New Babylonian handlers. At that moment they became demon energy. But the Sword of Methuselah killed them and their energy like a wand from God. In a strange merciful way, the Sword of Methuselah was releasing the demons from their torment. And as God's chosen man, Angus scythed them to death. It appeared as though the demons were sacrificing themselves, to be gone forever in order to save themselves from their torments. Angus became the mad harvester of the profane, gathering the already dead and giving them eternal rest, ridding their kind from the planet.

Sir Richardson and Sir Palin kept close to Grand Master de Molay, each knight putting his hand on the shoulder of the knight next to him. They were an impregnable wall of protection for the deadliest weapon ever wielded against evil. Sometimes the knights were flesh, sometimes the stone in their essence lived and died, transmuting through dimensional reality, as the antidote to what had come to pass in London. They lived through all the ancient battles and had triumphed over themselves and their desires, becoming their own masters. For it was obvious the battle raged as much in the spiritual realms as in the reality of the now. Here, de Molay became more monk than Templar, praying in the middle of the wedge of stone knights, protecting Angus as he scythed the Sword of Methuselah against the wall of rats. As soon as the demon rats had been sliced in two, their green demon energy turned into a mist endeavouring to escape the Sword of Methuselah. The wall of rats continued to grow, changing from a wall structure to that of a wave which hung over the wedge of knights in suspended animation. From time to time, the essence of the demons broke into reality with a flicking tongue, a barbed claw, or indeed a contorted face, reminding all of their presence. Angus scythed on nevertheless with unnatural speed against them. The more rats that climbed the wall looking to drop onto the Grail Knights, the more were scythed back to where they'd come from. Angus had turned from man to a scything machine of God and now moved so fast he appeared like a supernatural Catherine wheel in the heat of Holy Light. The wall of rats lessened as more of the reptile demons were released. In many cases, releasing themselves, as the Sword of Methuselah swathed the wall to half its size. As the demons disappeared then so the power of the Saturn fallen angel began to shrink.

But who then, under these circumstances, could tell what was reality and what was not? People were now aware of the 'Battle for Reality', as so much of what had been known in London had changed. But like many, they'd drifted aimlessly without the comprehension of the war against them. This started with a whimpering of their own compliance, continuing incrementally till it raged against them. Many of them were dying in the streets.

No one could get a message through to the Grand Master as the wedge of stone Grail Knights were locked with the demon army, transmuted into the massive swarm of super rats. It was if they fought in some other dimension, flashing in and out of the reality of the now and the heavenly realms, locked betwixt both worlds in the 'Battle for Reality'.

The Templar Scientist Assumes Command

The Templar Scientist had been charged with taking the position of Grand Master in the case that de Molay died or became incapacitated in any way. Andrew Sinclair was the only knight who could now bestow this right upon him. With this in mind he walked over to the Templar Scientist with a solemn look.

"You are now Grand Master, you are therefore in command as we have always planned." Andrew Sinclair took off his purple robe, exposing his white Templar mantle. "I am first and foremost a Templar and you know what we must do next."

"Yes, I thought you'd say that. Well, I pray that my position is temporary and that our Grand Master returns; for now, he and Angus MacWilliam and the Grail Knights are somewhere between heaven and hell!"

The Holy Ark is Released

There was a silence in the Temple. The Holy Ark was held in the air six feet above the ground, vibrating gently. A dove landed above the chaos inside the Temple and looked down as if waiting for it to start up. All the people from London's dark streets who had not complied with evil, stood round the inside perimeter of the Temple looking up at the dove. Children cried, soothed temporarily by their brave parents who had brought them to safety.

The acting Grand Master nodded his head at Andrew Sinclair, who in turn nodded over to the main Priest of the Holy Ark and gave him the key of the Grail bowl. There was a place outside of the Holy Ark where the Grail should be suspended. And so the Ark roared into life, slowing down to a steady pulsating energy. It levitated higher on its catafalque borne by the High Priests, and they rose with it appearing as if they were walking down a desert path in some other place. The same thing had happened when the Philistines stole the ark but had to return it after it destroyed half of their army. They were the same Priests, in their special purple robes, who had trodden the desert to get it back then.

Now they brought it forth in the same way. Although this time it was being taken into the streets of London as it was a spiritual desert for those gone over to the bad. All the people watched as it was carried out. As it went by anyone who had been marked by the Saturn entity were released from their electronic servitude to it. Many collapsed freed from the malignancy which had inhabited them. The Ark facilitated the direct action of God curing the people as it passed them by. The Ark and it's High Priests were contained under a clear dome of illuminated ether. A gentle desert breeze from two thousand years ago ruffled their purple robes as if they were living in two ages at the same time. As they left the Temple, instead of the people giving up for the benefit of short-term security, they walked behind it and more of their kind, both the marked and the unmarked street people came and joined the procession. Those that followed the Holy Ark were healed for it could see the truth and the truth set them free.

Soon Andrew Sinclair and the acting Grand Master could see the centre of the battle against the Saturn entity and the quickly diminishing wall of rats. Thus releasing the demons from their torment and assigning them to oblivion rather than hell. On seeing their peace more of their kind consigned themselves to the same fate. And as they did the power of the Saturn entity shrank in its planes of existence, from its fake electronic dimension to the one now, which it had attempted to take over to control mankind and planet Earth. The Ark, followed by the people grouped around in front of this faceless entity, as now the awesome power of God came directly against it. These people inadvertently imbued the Ark with a jolt of extra power and it began to pulse out a Sacred Light in the form of millions of bees. The intense ray blasted the middle of the Saturn entity with this manifestation, and it began to crumble, like the walls of Jericho. Meanwhile the bees, those holy insects, were seen inside the Saturn stinging away. As they stung so it's demonic energy shrank away. Angus MacWilliam scythed on, never once stopping, until all that remained of the wall of rats was a million tails forming the numbers 1717, the indefatigable number of God. Finally, having wielded the Sword of Methuselah against the demon army non-stop, until it was defeated, could Angus rest.

The wedge of the Grail Knights backed away slowly as the Holy Ark, carried by its Priests processed against the Saturn entity, which diminished from a colossus, to a giant, and finally to the size of a man.

Angus sheathed the Sword of Methuselah and fell to the ground exhausted. The Saturn entity now stood weak and shrunken oscillating between one fake life and another, surrounded by two million people. The marked and unmarked had come together to take back their country and lives. Back from his trauma, Grand Master de Molay started the final actions against their enemies. Laura Bellamy had captured their Supreme Accountant, also known as the Whore of Babylon. She was brought forward at cutlass point and forced to stand next to what remained of the thing that had controlled her and her political career. The Saturn entity's inner workings of microchips and fake blood reverted to a mere two-dimensional manifestation of weakness and wrong, no more powerful than the fear of the people from which it had been enabled. All that remained of the two evil forces was a pair of worn-out husks like two aged dung beetles.

The people of London, in all their forms and types moved closer, finally realising what had been happening. Above them the giant dragonfly, stationed on the utilities building, shrank back to a normal size and flickered down around them, bringing a sense of spiritual transition. The pair of defunct souls, once leaders of evil watched as its beautiful shadow passed over them. They collapsed to their knees, defeated in every way that was possible. London woke up after taking stock of what had happened and knowing they had played a part in assisting evil against themselves, but were now helping to rectify that.

The giant ants and their riders disappeared back to where they'd come from. Not through tunnels and extreme weather but back through spiritual portals; back to where they could guard the nether regions of Antarctica. The scorpion-tailed locusts turned into gold leafed ornamentations decorating buildings near the scene. Those sacred beasts which had come to the assistance of the good transformed back to the stone gargoyles they had once been. The stone Grail Knights, having done their job, marched slowly back to the Temple still flickering with power betwixt reality and molecular energy. Angus marched with them exhausted and feeling like death was near. The Templars and the pirates, as the Army of God gathered together and marched down the ethereal path of the spirit, back to where they had come from.

The destruction all over London reverted back to an earlier time of prosperity. The marble casing of the Houses of Babylon fell, crumbling into dust and blowing away. Parliament was still there but now things had finally changed. The false gods which had been installed where Big Ben had been, evaporated into nothingness and that great clock and symbol of a better time returned to its former glory.

Only a solitary rat remained in the all-pervasive good energy around. It looked up and scurried past the million rat tails, which formed the name of God known as the Tetragrammaton, back into the sewers from whence it came. A dramatic silence fell upon the city.

From the Octagonal Tower

Meanwhile, the hunched over figure of Andrew Sinclair could be seen writing in his Octagonal study overlooking the River Thames, whilst his concierge went about his everyday business, hanging keys up and delivering letters. No one knew what Andrew Sinclair had been writing or why. He went over to a bottle of Châteauneuf-du-Pape and poured himself a large glass. If someone had been looking over from the other side of the river, they would have seen his tiny silhouette downing it in one and brushing back his quiff ready to pour another.

If you'd been in the room with him, you would have heard him saying goodbye to the Grand Master of the Knights Templar, Jacques de Molay, simultaneously saluting by holding his right hand over his heart.

"Until next time Grand Master," as he ceased to write and started to drink the potent life force of the grape. As he did, another hand appeared on the wall behind him. It was a white hand similar to the hand of Leonardo da Vinci and it wrote on the wall in an unknown language. The writing said that the New Babylonians had been weighed and found wanting by God and that already another Empire would rise to destroy them.

Meanwhile all had reverted back to normal in the Temple. The stone effigies of the Grail Knights were back in position, lying recumbent on the stone flags in all their accustomed glory. Their legs bent signifying their symbolic heroism. They grasped their swords carved in stone; fearless knights of Britain who had lived and died in the service of God. All of them had redeemed themselves and by their mighty actions were penitent no more.

One of them, though, differed. His armour was segmented like the body of a pangolin and he wore a shell like helmet and carried a shorter curved sword. It was as if he was from further back in antiquity, yet remained one of them. For Angus MacWilliam had been one of those warrior masons, who had rebuilt the walls of Jerusalem, sword in one hand and trowel in the other. They had been the forerunners of the Knights Templar.

Looking down on the thirteen knights, a man in Templar mantle, with a cross denominating his rank as Grand Master, was seen entering an upper room in the Temple Church. Jacques de Molay had one last thing to do. He snuffed out a burning candle in its medieval candlestick, which had burned brightly on the Altar of God for the duration of the biggest battle for the souls of humanity ever on the streets of London. As he did so the twelve pairs of stone eyes of the Grail Knights finally closed, at rest for now. But in the all-pervasive peace, one knight's eyes remained wide open, consigned by God to watch over his fellow Brethren for all eternity, seemingly now stone but like the rest of his brothers, his heart beat on.

Angus MacWilliam had finally earned the trust of God to watch over the Grail Knights as they slept until they were needed once again to save mankind. As the doves returned to the peace of the Temple, all movement ceased save the beating hearts of the Grail Knights, waiting and watching in stone for the next rising of the Armies of God...

The Battle Begins Again

But then a voice rang out in the silence. *"Come back Angus we've not quite finished. You forgot something. Remember Loch Eriboll and that bleak house down there?"* There was a silence which could only be described as grey. As grey as those foreboding waters which lay around that mysterious house below the stone walls of Eriboll. Although Angus was transmuting into stone his effigy could still hear Andrew Sinclair. *"Go back there, for God's sake Angus go back there. I will meet you where the waters meet the steps."* Although unable to speak, Angus thought the words in his mind's eye.

"Och' Andrew, there's always something else, always another twist to fathom but right enough I'll go there, but now I must sleep." Above Angus in the Temple Church, the dove which had waited flew up and away through the blades of light pouring in through the gothic windows. The blades of light turned to fingers and an illuminated hand formed from them. It moved as if writing over the vellum of eternity. The dove flew to the vision of the hand and disappeared…